U0025463

5

Alice's Adventures in Wonderland

愛麗絲夢遊仙境

Original Author   Lewis Carroll
Adaptor   Norman Fung
Proofreaders   Dennis Le Boeuf / Liming Jing

WORDS
1000

MP3

Let's Enjoy Masterpieces!

All the beautiful fairy tales and masterpieces that you have encountered during your childhood remain as warm memories in your adulthood. This time, let's indulge in the world of masterpieces through English. You can enjoy the depth and beauty of original works, which you can't enjoy through Chinese translations.

The stories are easy for you to understand because of your familiarity with them. When you enjoy reading, your ability to understand English will also rapidly improve.

This series of *Let's Enjoy Masterpieces* is a special reading comprehension booster program, devised to improve reading comprehension for beginners whose command of English is not satisfactory, or who are elementary, middle, and high school students. With this program, you can enjoy reading masterpieces in English with fun and efficiency.

This carefully planned program is composed of 5 levels, from the beginner level of 350 words to the intermediate and advanced levels of 1,000 words. With this program's level-by-level system, you are able to read famous texts in English and to savor the true pleasure of the world's language.

The program is well conceived, composed of reader-friendly explanations of English expressions and grammar, quizzes to help the student learn vocabulary and understand the meaning of the texts, and fabulous illustrations that adorn every page. In addition, with our "Guide to Listening," not only is reading comprehension enhanced but also listening comprehension skills are highlighted.

In the audio recording of the book, texts are vividly read by professional American actors. The texts are rewritten, according to the levels of the readers by an expert editorial staff of native speakers, on the basis of standard American English with the ministry of education recommended vocabulary. Therefore, it will be of great help even for all the students that want to learn English.

Please indulge yourself in the fun of reading and listening to English through *Let's Enjoy Masterpieces*.

HOW TO USE THIS BOOK
本書使用說明

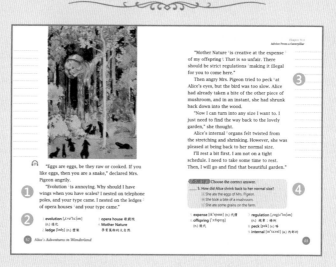

1 Original English texts

It is easy to understand the meaning of the text, because the text is rewritten according to the levels of the readers.

2 Explanation of the vocabulary

The words and expressions that include vocabulary above the elementary level are clearly defined.

3 Response notes

Spaces are included in the book so you can take notes about what you don't understand or what you want to remember.

4 Check Up

Review quizzes to check you understanding of the text.

🎧 *Audio Recording*

In the audio recording, native speakers narrate the texts in standard American English. By combining the written words and the audio recording, you can listen to English with great ease.

Audio books have been popular in Britain and America for many decades. They allow the listener to experience the proper word pronunciation and sentence intonation that add important meaning and drama to spoken English. Students will benefit from listening to the recording twenty or more times.

After you are familiar with the text and recording, listen once more with your eyes closed to check your listening comprehension. Finally, after you can listen with your eyes closed and understand every word and every sentence, you are then ready to mimic the native speaker.

Then you should make a recording by reading the text yourself. Then play both recordings to compare your oral skills with those of a native speaker.

HOW TO IMPROVE READING ABILITY

如何增進英文閱讀能力

① *Catch key words*

Read the key words in the sentences and practice catching the gist of the meaning of the sentence. You might question how working with a few important words could enhance your reading ability. However, it's quite effective.   If you continue to use this method, you will find out that the key words and your knowledge of people and situations enables you to understand the sentence.

② *Divide long sentences*

Read in chunks of meaning, dividing sentences into meaningful chunks of information. In the book, chunks are arranged in sentences according to meaning. If you consider the sentences backwards or grammatically, your reading speed will be slow and you will find it difficult to listen to English.

You are ready to move to a more sophisticated level of comprehension when you find that narrowly focusing on chunks is irritating. Instead of considering the chunks, you will make it a habit to read the sentence from the beginning to the end to figure out the meaning of the whole.

❸ Make inferences and assumptions

Making inferences and assumptions is part of your ability. If you don't know, try to guess the meaning of the words. Although you don't know all the words in context, don't go straight to the dictionary. Developing an ability to make inferences in the context is important.

The first way to figure out the meaning of a word is from its context. If you cannot make head or tail out of the meaning of a word, look at what comes before or after it. Ask yourself what can happen in such a situation. Make your best guess as to the word's meaning. Then check the explanations of the word in the book or look up the word in a dictionary.

❹ Read a lot and reread the same book many times

There is no shortcut to mastering English. Only if you do a lot of reading will you make your way to the summit. Read fun and easy books with an average of less than one new word per page. Try to immerse yourself in English as often as you can.

Spend time "swimming" in English. Language learning research has shown that immersing yourself in English will help you improve your English, even though you may not be aware of what you're learning.

CONTENTS

Chapter One

🎧₁ # Down the Rabbit Hole

It was a lazy spring day; crickets were calling. Alice and her older sister were down by the river. Her sister was deeply involved[1] in reading a magazine featuring[2] Indian poets.

Alice wanted to use daisies[3] to make a chain[4] for her cat Dinah. She asked her sister to help, but her sister replied with an abrupt[5] "No!"

1. **involve** in [ɪnˈvɑːlv] (v.) 使專注；使忙於
2. **feature** [ˈfiːtʃər] (v.) 以……為特色
3. **daisy** [ˈdeɪzi] (n.) 雛菊
4. **chain** [tʃeɪn] (n.) 項圈
5. **abrupt** [əˈbrʌpt] (a.) 突然的
6. **consistent** [kənˈsɪstət] (a.) 前後一致的
7. **wander off** 閒逛；漫遊
8. **droopy** [ˈdruːpɪ] (a.) 下垂的
9. **whisker** [ˈwɪskər] (n.) 鬍鬚
10. **exclaim** [ɪkˈskleɪm] (n.) 驚叫
11. **noteworthy** [ˈnoʊtˌwɜːrði] (a.) 值得注意的

The sudden reaction was consistent[6] with her sister's character. She always turned mean whenever her reading was interrupted. Alice wandered off[7] on her own.

Suddenly, a white male rabbit stopped in front of Alice. He wore a tight jacket. "Oh, my droopy[8] ears and split whiskers[9]! I am late!" Mr. White Rabbit exclaimed[10] while looking at his watch.

"A rabbit that could tell time is surely a mystery," Alice said to herself. She thought a rabbit with such noteworthy[11] intelligence would be a supremely interesting subject for a story, a tale that would greatly impress her friends.

Alice called out, "Oh, Mr. Rabbit!"

But Mr. Rabbit ran away, crying, "Oh, dear! I am late!"

Burning with curiosity, Alice chased after him.

Check Up Choose the correct answer.

T
F
1. A male rabbit appeared in front of Alice while she was wandering alone.

_____ 2. Why did Alice follow Mr. Rabbit?
A She thought a rabbit that could tell time would be a great story to tell her friends.
B She was suspicious of Mr. Rabbit.
C She wanted to save Mr. Rabbit from some bad guys.

11

Mr. Rabbit suddenly stopped to part[1] the grass at the root of a tree and expose[2] a rabbit hole. He gave Alice a quick wave of his paw[3] as a visual signal and an indication[4] that she should follow him.

In a bid[5] to show her courage, Alice jumped into the hole right after Mr. Rabbit. The rabbit-hole dropped vertically[6], and Alice felt as if she were falling down a very deep well.

Alice fell past a large map of the British Empire. She imagined falling through the earth to Australia. As a tourist in a remote and far away country, she thought it would be her honor to give those Australians a demonstration[7] of proper manners.

She tried to practice curtsying[8] while falling, but she couldn't do it because it was simply too difficult to make a curtsy while dropping through the air.

1. **part** [pɑːrt] (v.) 使分開
2. **expose** [ɪkˈspoʊ] (v.) 使暴露於
3. **paw** [pɔː] (n.) （動物）腳爪
4. **indication** [ˌɪndɪˈkeɪʃən] (n.) 表示；指示
5. **bid** [bɪd] (n.) 企圖；努力
6. **vertically** [ˈvɜːrtɪkli] (adv.) 垂直地
7. **demonstration** [ˌdemənˈstreɪʃən] (n.) 示範
8. **curtsy** [ˈkɜːrtsi] (v.) 行屈膝禮

"What if I end up in a cave full of bats[1]?" That thought filled Alice with anxiety. "There are widespread[2] news reports about such caves in some parts of Australia. Oh, I wish Dinah were here."

Alice loved having her cat Dinah in her bedroom in the day or at night to guarantee that no mouse would come sneaking[3] around. Alice strongly believed that bats were simply mice that learned how to fly. If Dinah were here, she would be able to reassure[4] Alice in any Australian cave, even one filled with bats.

"However, Dinah likes to stay at home," Alice thought. "Well, for Dinah's sake[5], it is better that she isn't falling with me."

✔ Check Up True or False

T
F 3. Alice gave a demonstration of curtsy to those Australians.

1. **bat** [bæt] (n.) 蝙蝠
2. **widespread** [ˈwaɪdspred] (a.) 散佈廣的
3. **sneak** [sniːk] (v.) 偷偷地走
4. **reassure** [ˌriə'ʃʊr] (v.) 使放心
5. **for someone's sake** 為了某人好

At last, Alice landed on a huge pile of twigs[1] and dry leaves, neatly placed there so that they could gently break[2] the fall of anyone who came dropping down out of the rabbit hole.

She could see Mr. Rabbit running up ahead at a very fast pace[3], and she hurriedly chased after him. Soon, she ran into a room with numerous[4] doors. The room was built in the style of Victorian architecture[5]. Mr. Rabbit was no longer to be seen, and all the doors were locked.

Alice saw a table, and on it were a golden key and a bottle with a label that said "DRINK ME." The key opened a tiny steel door, but it was too small for Alice to go through. The steel[6] door was an entrance[7] to a beautiful garden.

1. **twig** [twɪg] (n.) 樹枝
2. **break** [breɪk] (v.) 中止旅程
3. **pace** [peɪs] (n.) 步速
4. **numerous** [ˈnjuːmərəs] (a.) 許多的
5. **Victorian architecture** 19到20世紀初維多利亞時期建築
6. **steel** [stiːl] (n.) 鋼鐵
7. **entrance** [ˈentrəns] (n.) 入口

Without thinking, she shut the door and locked it. She put the key back on the table and opened the bottle.

Alice sniffed[8] at the bottle to make sure it did not contain any alcohol, because children should not drink alcohol. It did not contain any alcohol, and Alice became curious about the taste of the liquid.

"A mere[9] drop won't kill me." Alice popped open the bottle and took a sip . . . then another. It tasted good and had the distinct[10] flavor of tart[11] cherries. Then she drank the entire bottle.

To her surprise, she began to shrink. The liquid in the bottle was a formula[12] to shrink bodies.

8. **sniff** [snɪf] (v.) 嗅；聞
9. **mere** [mɪr] (a.) 僅僅的
10. **distinct** [dɪˈstɪŋkt] (a.) 明顯的
11. **tart** [tɑːrt] (n.) 水果餡餅
12. **formula** [ˈfɔːmjələ] (n.) 配方

"Too bad my sister is not here to witness[1] this extraordinary transformation[2]. It seems as if extraordinary things are simply routine[3] events today," Alice made the cheerful remark[4] while watching her body become smaller and smaller.

"What if I shrink[5] down to nothing? That would be a disaster[6]!" Suddenly she became very worried.

Alice would not let her fears defeat[7] her spirit. She tried to overcome her worry by saying a prayer. Suddenly she stopped shrinking.

1. **witness** [ˈwɪtnɪs] (v.) 見證
2. **transformation** [ˌtrænsfərˈmeɪʃən] (n.) 變化;轉變
3. **routine** [ruːˈtiːn] (n.) 例行公事
4. **remark** [rɪˈmɑrk] (n.) 評論
5. **shrink** [ʃrɪnk] (v.) 縮小
6. **disaster** [dɪˈzæstəʴ] (n.) 災難
7. **defeat** [dɪˈfiːt] (v|) 擊敗

She was now only a few inches tall and just the right size for going through the little door into that lovely garden.

However, she was too small to reach up for the key on the table.

"Where is Mr. Rabbit? Is there anyone here to help me?" she asked helplessly.

Then she spotted[8] a small glass box that was lying under the table. She opened the box and found a very small cake in it. On the cake the words "EAT ME" were marked in currants[9]. She took a bite of it without thinking twice.

✓ Check Up Choose the correct answer.

T 4. Alice found out that there was some alcohol in the bottle.

F 5. What did Alice eat after drinking the bottle of potion?

_____

8 **spot** [spɑːt] (v.) 察覺   9. **currant** [ˈkɜːrənt] (n.) 葡萄乾

Chapter Two

6

The Pool of Tears

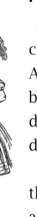

The cake made Alice's body grow. In a second, her head was pressing against the ceiling. She was now more than nine feet tall! Alice easily picked up the key from the table, but she was now too big to get through the tiny door. Frustrated, she lowered herself by lying down.

Then she heard a little pattering[1] of feet in the distance and saw Mr. Rabbit returning, with a big fan in one hand.

Desperate[2], Alice was ready to ask help from anyone. "Help! Mr. White Rabbit, please help me!" Alice tried to stop Mr. Rabbit, but he dropped his large fan and scuttled[3] past her.

✓ Check Up

1. What was left behind when Mr. Rabbit scuttled past Alice?

_____

1. **patter** ['pætər] (v.)
   跑步啪嗒聲

2. **desperate** ['despərɪt]
   (a.) 危急的；絕望的

3. **scuttle** ['skʌtl] (v.) 小步快跑

Alice tried to pick up the fan, but her huge arm was too big a burden. Even a small movement required great concentration[1] and effort. Alice felt like a disabled[2] person; her feet were too far away from her body.

"If I grow any bigger, I will have to buy new shoes and mail them to my feet." She realized the idea was absurd[3].

"Am I dreaming? Am I conscious[4]? Am I still myself?" She felt as if her brain was working very slowly and she was as confused as her friend Mabel.

"I am not Mabel, and I can prove it! I am a more advanced learner than she is. I know that salaries[5] in England are paid in Singaporean dollars, and salaries in France are paid in Japanese yen[6]. "

"Wait! That can't be correct! Professionals[7] in all kinds of occupations[8] would be very confused. All their paychecks and bank accounts would be in foreign languages. Furthermore, their pay would not be accurate."

1. **concentration** [ˌkɑːnsənˈtreɪʃən] (n.) 專心
2. **disabled** [dɪsˈeɪbəld] (a.) 殘障的

3. **absurd** [əbˈsɜːrd] (a.) 荒謬的
4. **conscious** [ˈkɑːnʃəs] (a.) 神智清醒的

"Still, maybe a small percentage of the population would be happy with Singaporean dollars and Japanese yen. Merchants could increase the price of oil, wheat, and rice."

"Because of all this confusion about money, some people would even think copper[9] is gold and silver is platinum[10]. Fortunes would be quickly made and lost, because no one would be sure of the price of anything."

"My goodness, I am Mabel! And if I really am her, I have no father, live in poverty, have the worst conduct[11] at school, and know nothing about economics. Oh me, oh my! How silly can I be? Why does everything seem to be at least half of a lie?"

5. **salary** [ˈsæləri] (n.) 薪水
6. **yen** [jen] (n.) 日圓
7. **professional** [prəˈfeʃənəl] (n.) 專家
8. **occupation** [ˌɑːkjəˈpeɪʃən] (n.) 工作；職位
9. **copper** [ˈkɑːpər] (n.) 銅
10. **platinum** [ˈplætɪnəm] (n.) 白金
11. **conduct** [ˈkəndʌkt] (n.) 品行

✔ Check Up　Choose the correct answer.

_____ 2. What school subject was Mabel weak at?
    Ⓐ Economics
    Ⓑ Mathematics
    Ⓒ Physical Education
    Ⓓ French

Her soul searching gave her no satisfaction[1]. Very worried, Alice started to cry. Giant tears rolled down her cheeks like waterfalls. Mr. Rabbit's fan was now floating[2]. She managed to pick up the fan and started fanning herself, because she suddenly felt very hot.

"Isn't there anyone here to give me some guidance[3]? Where is the landlord of this place? I don't deserve[4] to have such a diminutive[5] mind trying to control my massive[6] body."

1. **satisfaction** [ˌsætɪsˈfækʃən] (n.) 滿意;滿足;愉快
2. **float** [floʊt] (v.) 漂浮
3. **guidance** [ˈgaɪdəns] (n.) 指導
4. **deserve** [dɪˈzɜːrv] (v.) 應得
5. **diminutive** [dɪˈmɪnjʊtɪv] (a.) 微小的
6. **massive** [ˈmæsɪv] (a.) 巨大的

Alice continued shedding tears[7]. "I need a consultant[8], someone to tell me how to manage this awful confusion about my true identity."

She kept fanning[9] herself as she went on talking, "I wish my dear sister were here as my adviser. She could give me some proof that I am not Mabel. I am so tired of being all alone here!"

Suddenly, Alice found herself shrinking. Soon she was small again. Her fanning had shrunk her body. She dropped the fan hastily[10] in order to avoid shrinking to nothingness.

She thought, "Wow! I could have ended up without any body at all. I had a narrow escape[11] from a strange situation! I am so lucky!"

✓ Check Up

3. What did Alice do to make her tiny again?

_____

7. **shed tears** 流眼淚；哭泣
8. **consultant** [kən'sʌltənt] (n.) 顧問
9. **fan** [fæn] (v.) 用扇子扇
10. **hastily** ['heɪstɪli] (adv.) 匆忙地
11. **narrow escape** 千鈞一髮地脫險

Then an unexpected wave swept Alice off her feet, and she found herself up to her chin in salt water. She was about to drown[1] in a torrent[2] of her own tears, which she had shed when she was nine feet tall!

"I wish I had not cried so much!" Alice said, as she swam about, trying to find a way out of the flood.

"Hey, you!" someone shouted in a very high pitch. There was a silhouette[3] of a mouse swimming on a distant wave. Most bats were great at flying, and common mice were outstanding[4] swimmers.

Being with a great swimmer, even if it was a mouse, would greatly enhance[5] Alice's chances of survival. Drowning was not a good option[6], so Alice swam toward the mouse with determination[7].

1. **drown** [draʊn] (v.) 淹死
2. **torrent** [ˈtɑːrənt] (n.) 奔流
3. **silhouette** [ˌsɪluˈet] (n.) 側面剪影
4. **outstanding** [ˈaʊtˈstændɪŋ] (a.) 傑出的
5. **enhance** [ɪnˈhæns] (v.) 增加

6. **option** [ˈɑːpʃən] (n.) 選擇
7. **determination** [dɪˌtɜːrmɪˈneɪʃən] (n.) 果斷；決心
8. **fur** [fɜːr] (n.) （動物的）軟毛
9. **vessel** [ˈvesəl] (n.) 船艦

"Pull on my fur[8] to climb onto my back," Mr. Mouse suggested.

Alice buried her fingers into Mr. Mouse's fur and clambered up.

She was quite tired and very grateful that Mr. Mouse was willing to become her vessel[9].

✓ Check Up Choose the correct answer.

T 4. Alice escaped from the flood of her tears by climbing
F   up on a metal vessel.

27

"You paddle[1] well for a little girl. Your swim was impressive. You swam quite swell[2] over every swell[3]," Mr. Mouse declared[4].

"Thank you for your compliments[5]! I swam without reserve, because I was afraid of drowning," Alice said.

Full of confidence, Mr. Mouse emphatically[6] stated, "We'll soon reach the shore."

Alice replied, "Really? I don't see any land up ahead."

"Are you questioning my judgment?" Mr. Mouse snapped[7].

"No," Alice murmured[8]. She had not yet recovered her breath from swimming and didn't want to cause any problems.

"Speak louder, please. I am old, and my ears are aged. I can't even hear myself very well," snapped Mr. Mouse. "Are you afraid of a live mouse?"

1. **paddle** [ˈpædəl] (v.) 用槳划船，此指在水裡游得很好
2. **swell** [swel] (adv.) 極好地
3. **swell** (n.) 波濤
4. **declare** [dɪˈkler] (v.) 宣稱；表示
5. **compliment** [ˈkɑːplɪmənt] (n.) 讚美
6. **emphatically** [ɪmˈfætɪkli] (adv.) 強調地
7. **snap** [snæp] (v.) 厲聲說
8. **murmur** [ˈmɜːrmər] (v.) 低聲說
9. **rodent** [ˈroʊdənt] (n.) 齧齒目動物

"Usually I am, but Dinah keeps rodents[9] away from me," Alice told Mr. Mouse.

"Who is Dinah?" he asked.

"My cat," she replied.

"I hate cats! They are despicable[10] creatures[11]," he declared angrily.

"I beg to differ; my Dinah is adorable . . . "

"Don't lecture[12] me about adorable cats," Mr. Mouse snapped again.

He paused for a few seconds and then asked, "Would you like cats if you were me?"

"I guess not. You and I are both a bit small and insignificant[13] in the big universe[14]."

✓ Check Up

5. Who was Dinah, and how did she protect Alice back home?

_____

10. **despicable** [dɪ'spɪkəbəl] (a.)
可惡的；卑鄙的
11. **creature** ['kriːtʃər] (n.) 生物
12. **lecture** ['lektʃər]
(v.) 向……演講

13. **insignificant**
[ˌɪnsɪg'nɪfɪkənt]
(a.) 無足輕重的
14. **universe** ['juːnɪvɜːrs]
(n.) 宇宙；全世界

"If Dinah were here, she might not recognize me and she might even chase me away or do something worse," Alice replied in a voice filled with some genuine[1] sympathy[2] and empathy[3].

Then she said with enthusiasm[4], "You are such a great swimmer! We must be getting close to the shore!" Alice hoped her enthusiastic compliment on his swimming would help to change the subject of their conversation."

Willy Pogány.

Clearly there was a lack of appreciation[5] among rats, mice, and bats of any adorable cat that loves to hunt. Making a speech concerning Dinah's clever and lovely qualities would be pointless[6] and foolish in her current situation.

"To be precise, we have twelve more feet to swim," said Mr. Mouse. Then he counted off every foot for Alice.

✓ Check Up Choose the correct answer.

T
F　6. Alice suddenly became enthusiastic because she hoped to change the topic of the conversation.

1. **genuine** ['dʒenjuɪn] (a.) 真誠的
2. **sympathy** ['sɪmpəθi] (n.) 同情
3. **empathy** ['empəθi] (n.) 同理心
4. **enthusiasm** [ɪn'θjuːziæzəm] (n.) 熱情

5. **appreciation** [əˌpriːʃɪ'eɪʃən] (n.) 欣賞
6. **pointless** ['pɔɪntləs] (a.) 無意義的

31

Chapter Three

🎧 12

The Caucus Race and a Long Tale

Alice noticed some movement on the shore. An array of strange creatures became visible[1] as Alice's eyes got used to the darkness. It was indeed a queer[2]-looking group of birds and animals that had gathered on the bank[3]. All of them looked wet, cold, and uncomfortable.

"Come join us," said Ms. Dodo Bird, and her soprano[4] voice seemed very musical. Alice and Mr. Mouse accepted the invitation.

They huddled[5] alongside each other for warmth and comfort. Silence fell. They kept their activities to the minimum in order to conserve[6] their energy.

1. **visible** ['vɪzɪbəl] (a.) 可見的
2. **queer** [kwɪr] (a.) 古怪的
3. **bank** [bæŋk] (n.) 堤岸
4. **soprano** [sə'prænoʊ] (n.) 女高音
5. **huddle** ['hʌdl] (v.) 聚在一起
6. **conserve** [kən'sɜ:rv] (v.) 保存

Mr. Mouse, with his dominant[1] personality, broke the silence to suggest a way to get everyone <u>dry</u>. His tone shifted[2], and his voice became deep for an announcement:

"History is always exceedingly[3] <u>dry</u>. A story about good old England will certainly get rid of all our wetness." Mr. Mouse assumed[4] the air of an historian as he began a long story about history.

"The holy Pope favored William's cause of conquering[5] the people north of the channel. Thus, William the Conqueror thought that God, the operator of miracles and mysteries, endorsed[6] his mission. As he marched into London, he found it necessary to . . . "

"Found what?" Mrs. Duck asked, and her question upset Mr. Mouse.

"Found 'it,'" he replied angrily. "Don't you know what 'it' refers to?" Mr. Mouse growled[7], and Mrs. Duck didn't dare to repeat her question.

1. **dominant** ['dɑːmɪnənt] (a.) 支配的
2. **shift** [ʃɪft] (v.) 轉變
3. **exceedingly** [ɪkˈsiːdɪŋli] (adv.) 極度地
4. **assume** [əˈsuːm] (v.) 裝出
5. **conquer** [ˈkɑːŋkər] (v.) 攻克
6. **endorse** [ɪnˈdɔːrs] (v.) 贊同
7. **growl** [graʊl] (v.) 咆哮
8. **whine** [waɪn] (v.) 發牢騷
9. **solemnly** [ˈsɑːləmli] (adv.) 嚴肅地
10. **resign** [rɪˈzaɪn] (v.) 辭去
11. **trill** [trɪl] (v.) 鳥啼囀

"We are still as wet as ever," Mrs. Duck whined[8].

Mr. Mouse solemnly[9] declared, "All right, I resign[10] from the task of drying out all of you!" Then he turned away from the wet crowd.

"Let's dry ourselves by doing some sports," Ms. Dodo trilled[11].

"Good idea! Let's form two teams," Mr. Lory Bird suggested.

"No, no. No opponents[12]. Let's have a Caucus Race[13]," Ms. Dodo trilled again. Everyone cheered, and even Mr. Mouse was satisfied with Ms. Dodo's idea.

✓ Check Up

1. What are the meanings of the word **"dry"** underlined in the first and second paragraph on page 34?

   _____

2. What did the animals do to try to dry themselves?

   _____

---

12. **opponent** [əˈpoʊnənt]
    (n.) 對手;敵手

13. **Caucus Race** 會議式賽跑
    Caucus是指「黨團會議」,
    這裡是「嘲諷黨團會議的複
    雜性」

They milled around[1] and drew a strange shape as a racecourse[2].

"But there is only one lane!" Alice felt something was not quite right.

Mrs. Duck explained, "Use the brain God gave you. Be creative. You are supposed to find your own path in life. So, use your imagination to find your own lane."

"But I . . . "

"Should we ban[3] her from this race?" Mrs. Duck interrupted[4] Alice.

Everyone consulted with Ms. Dodo, who finally announced, "No. Everyone should participate in the race. She will find her own lane."

Ms. Dodo then gave the clue "the opposite of end," by which she meant "begin."

1. **mill around** 成群地亂轉
2. **racecourse** ['reɪskɔːrs] (n.) 跑道
3. **ban** [bæn] (v.) 禁止
4. **interrupt** [ˌɪntəˈrʌpt] (v.) 打斷某人說話
5. **participant** [pɑːrˈtɪsəpənt] (n.) 參與者
6. **inevitable** [ɪˈnevɪtəbəl] (a.) 必然的
7. **descend into** (v.) 陷入
8. **chaos** [ˈkeɪɑːs] (n.) 混亂
9. **shrug** [ʃrʌg] (v.) 聳肩（表示疑惑）

Immediately all the participants[5] began bumping into each other. It was inevitable[6] that the race descended into[7] chaos[8].

When everyone became too tired to run or bump into anyone, Ms. Dodo declared, "The race is over; we all won. Now who has the prizes?" Everyone shrugged[9] except for Alice.

✓ Check Up   Choose the correct answer.

T
F   3. Nobody won the Caucus Race except Alice.

"I have some candy." Alice pulled out a box of candy from her pocket, and luckily all the candies were dry. She started to distribute[1] the pieces of candy, but there were not enough. Everyone had received one piece, except for Alice.

"She must have a prize, too," Mrs. Duck said.

Ms. Dodo asked Alice, "What else do you have in your pocket?"

"A thimble[2]," replied Alice.

"Hand it over to me," said Ms. Dodo, and she took Alice's thimble.

She carefully examined the thimble and then declared, "Even though you had this small cap of metal in your pocket, you did not own it. So, your reward[3] for participating in the race shall be the ownership of this elegant[4] thimble." Ms. Dodo spoke as if she were reciting[5] a poem.

1. **distribute** [dɪˈstrɪbjuːt] (v.) 分發
2. **thimble** [ˈθɪmbəl] (n.) 頂針
3. **reward** [rɪˈwɔːrd] (n.) 獎品
4. **elegant** [ˈelɪgənt] (a.) 優雅的
5. **recite** [rɪˈsaɪt] (v.) 朗誦

All the animals cheered. Alice thought the whole thing was very absurd[1], but she bowed solemnly[2] and took her thimble and put it back in her pocket.

Anyway, she was grateful for Ms. Dodo's suggestion of the race. All the animals had enjoyed the race and candy, and everyone was now dry.

"Now, I will tell you my story," Mr. Mouse spoke emphatically.

"Another story?" asked Mrs. Duck.

"We are dry now," Mr. Lory Bird commented[3]. Ignoring their comments, Mr. Mouse continued, "It is a long and sad tale . . ."

"Well, you certainly have a long tail, but how could a long tail be sad?" asked Alice. She was completely confused.

1. **absurd** [əb'sɜːrd] (a.) 荒謬的
2. **solemnly** ['sɑːləmli] (adv.) 正式地
3. **comment** ['kɑːment] (a.) 評論
4. **insult** [ɪn'sʌlt] (v.) 侮辱
5. **indignantly** [ɪn'dɪgnəntlɪ] (adv.) 憤怒地

"You insulted[4] me by talking such nonsense!" Mr. Mouse exclaimed indignantly[5]. "Goodbye!" he shouted and left without looking back.

"Please come back and finish your story," Alice called after Mr. Mouse, but there was no reply from Mr. Mouse.

"I wish Dinah were here to catch Mr. Mouse and bring him back to us," Alice said with a sigh.

"Who is Dinah?" asked Ms. Dodo.

"Dinah is my cat," explained Alice, "and she is excellent in catching mice. And oh, she is also very fast in going after bats and birds!"

✓ Check Up Choose the correct answer.

_____ 4. What did Alice get as her reward for winning the Caucus Race?

    Ⓐ A needle.

    Ⓑ A thimble.

    Ⓒ A piece of candy.

🎧 17

"Does Dinah eat birds?" asked Ms. Dodo, who was both confused and scared.

Alice quickly regretted her comment and said, "Oh, sorry. I forgot that you were a bird."

"You see, junior," Ms. Dodo screeched[1] to a young crab, "a little girl's spite[2] knows no limitations[3]. It is time for all of us to go home."

1. **screech** [skriːtʃ] (v.)
   發出尖銳的聲音
2. **spite** [spaɪt] (n.)
   心術不正；惡意
3. **limitation** [ˌlɪmɪˈteɪʃən] (n.) 極限
4. **pretext** [ˈpriːtekst] (n.)
   藉口；託辭
5. **patter** [ˈpætər] (v.)
   啪嗒啪嗒地響

Mrs. Duck told her little ducklings, "Come, my children; it is time for bed."

The old Magpie declared, "I really must be going home now; the night air doesn't suit my throat."

They all moved off on various pretexts[4]. Soon Alice was left alone. Feeling very lonely, she said to herself, "I wish I hadn't mentioned Dinah! Here, wherever here is, nobody seems to like cats. Oh, my poor Dinah!"

After a while, Alice again heard a little pattering[5] of footsteps, and she looked up eagerly, hoping Mr. Mouse was coming back to finish his story.

 Check Up

5. Why did the animals all leave?

_____

Chapter Four

🎧 18

The Rabbit and the Little Bill

All was quiet. Only the sound of pattering feet stirred in the air. Then, a familiar voice rang out and disturbed[1] the silence. It was Mr. White Rabbit, and he was mumbling[2] continuously.

"Where is my fan? I am late; the Duchess will have me executed[3]. Oh, she will be the architect of my demise[4] . . ."

When he saw Alice, he shouted at her with excitement, "Oh, Mary Ann, what are you doing out here? Be a good servant, and run home to fetch[5] my fan. Quick!"

1. **disturb** [dɪ'stɜːrb] (v.) 打擾
2. **mumble** ['mʌmbəl] (v.) 含糊地說
3. **execute** ['eksɪkjuːt] (v.) 處死
4. **demise** [dɪ'maɪz] (n.) 死亡
5. **fetch** [fetʃ] (v.) 拿來

"That will be my privilege[1], sir." Alice's acceptance of her new identity as Mr. Rabbit's servant was swift[2] and without hesitation[3].

As she ran off in the direction Mr. Rabbit had pointed, she thought with pride, "I can react quickly because I have a flexible mind."

Then she realized that she had entered a long corridor[4] that narrowed into almost a tube as she proceeded. She had to crawl[5] along, and finally she emerged[6] from a pipeline[7] into a farm on the summit of a small hill. The crops looked ripe for harvest.

Some cattle were grazing[8] by a house. On the door of the house was a bright brass plate with the name "W. RABBIT" engraved[9] upon it. Alice tapped on the door, but no one answered. She went in.

Inside the house, she saw some leather furniture. Instead of a fan, Alice found a little bottle. This time, there was no label with the words, "DRINK ME."

1. **privilege** [ˈprɪvəlɪdʒ] (n.) 個人的殊榮
2. **swift** [swɪft] (a.) 快速的
3. **hesitation** [ˌhezɪˈteɪʃən] (n.) 猶豫
4. **corridor** [ˈkɔːrɪdər] (n.) 狹長通道
5. **crawl** [krɔːl] (v.) 爬行
6. **emerge** [ɪˈmɜːrdʒ] (v.) 出現
7. **pipeline** [ˈpaɪplaɪn] (v.) 管道
8. **graze** [greɪz] (v.) 吃草
9. **engrave** [ɪnˈgreɪv] (v.) 雕刻；刻
10. **adjust** [əˈdʒʌst] (v.) 調整
11. **adapt** [əˈdæpt] (v.) 適應
12. **restrain** [rɪˈstreɪn] (v.) 限制；約束

"Something interesting is sure to happen,"
she said to herself, "whenever I eat or drink
something. I would like to see what this bottle
does. I hope it'll make me grow big again. I am
tired of being such a tiny little thing!" She
uncorked the bottle and began to drink.

So it did! Before she had finished half the
bottle, she found herself so big that her head
was pressing against the ceiling of Mr.
Rabbit's house.

She hastily put down the bottle and tried to
adjust[10] the positions of her arms and legs
and to adapt[11] to being in such a restraining[12]
space. She had to stick one arm out of the
window and one foot up the chimney.

Check Up Choose the correct answer.

T
F
1. Mr. Rabbit mistook Alice for his servant Mary Ann.

"Mary Ann! Mary Ann! Fetch my fan right now!" Alice heard Mr. Rabbit screaming outside the window.

"Bill! Bill the Lizard! Where are you?"

"Mr. Rabbit, my presence requested?" someone answered in broken grammar.

"That had to be Bill the Lizard," Alice thought.

"What is that in the window?" Mr. Rabbit asked.

"An arm that is, flesh and blood and all, evident it is," Bill replied.

"Well, it's got no business there. Get rid of it," Mr. Rabbit ordered.

Acting on instinct[1], Alice waved her arm and slapped[2] the two before Bill could do anything. They somersaulted[3] through the air and landed quite far away.

---

1. **instinct** [ˈɪnstɪŋkt] (n.) 本能
2. **slap** [slæp] (v.) 掌擊；拍
3. **somersault** [ˈsʌmərsɔːlt] (v.) 翻筋斗

Bill moaned[4], "Am I in heaven?" Apparently, the fall had badly injured him.

"Not yet," replied Mr. Rabbit while he was getting up from the ground. He dusted himself off and turned to the arm again. "We'll have to burn the house down!" he declared.

"If you come near me, I will send my cat Dinah after you," Alice shouted. A dead silence followed her threat.

"You can't use reason and logic[5] to communicate here," Alice thought. "The best thing to do is to make use of their fear of big animals. Maybe fear is the ultimate[6] law that governs everyone's psychology[7] and behavior."

✓ Check Up   Choose the correct answer.

_____ 2. What might be Bill's identity?
Ⓐ He is a lizard and Mr. Rabbit's neighbor.
Ⓑ He is a lizard and Mr. Rabbit's friend.
Ⓒ He is a lizard and Mr. Rabbit's servant.

T
F
3. Alice hit Mr. Rabbit and Bill because she thought the two were going to hurt her.

---

4. **moan** [moʊn] (v.) 嗚咽地說
5. **logic** [ˈlɑːdʒɪk] (n.) 邏輯

6. **ultimate** [ˈʌltɪmɪt] (a.) 最終的
7. **psychology** [saɪˈkɑːlədʒi] (n.) 心理學

🎧 21

Suddenly, Alice heard Mr. Rabbit shouting, "Aim . . . and fire!" A shower of little cakes came through the window. Alice swallowed one as quickly as possible, and she began to shrink, just as she had anticipated[1].

As soon as she was small enough to get through the door, she ran out of the house.

1. **anticipate** [ænˈtɪsɪpeɪt] (n.) 預期
2. **incident** [ˈɪnsɪdənt] (n.) 事件
3. **composition** [ˌkɑːmpəˈzɪʃən] (n.) 作文
4. **occasional** [əˈkeɪʒənəl] (a.) 偶爾的

"I will file all these incidents[2] into my memory," Alice thought while running away from the house.

"I will write a long composition[3] after I return to school, a summary of all these strange events. I'll explain the occasional[4], no, the constant confusion of identity I have suffered from."

"The advantages and disadvantages of being nine feet tall or a few inches tall should also be mentioned in my composition. But who will believe I am able to change my height from eating this and drinking that . . ."

✓ Check Up Choose the correct answer.

_____ 4. What were the "weapons" Mr. Rabbit used to attack Alice?

Ⓐ Cakes.

Ⓑ Stones.

Ⓒ Twigs.

Just then, in front of Alice appeared a huge puppy. The puppy was so big that it towered over Alice. It stretched out one paw, ready to touch her.

Desperate[1], Alice picked up a twig, which was heavy like a piece of lumber[2]. Using all her strength, she threw it as far as she could to distract[3] the puppy's attention.

The puppy turned, jumped into the air with a yelp[4] of delight[5], and chased after the twig. Alice seized the opportunity[6] to escape. After a long run, she collapsed[7] under a small bush to catch her breath.

Feeling safe enough, she started planning. "I have to grow to the right size, and I want to visit the garden behind the steel door." Her mind was set. She began looking for a bottle that might enlarge[8] her body one more time.

✓ Check Up

5. What did Alice determine to do after escaping from the dog?

_____

1. **desperate** [ˈdespərɪt] (a.) 情急拼命的
2. **lumber** [ˈlʌmbər] (n.) 木材
3. **distract** [dɪˈstrækt] (v.) 使分心
4. **yelp** [jelp] (n.) 狗吠聲
5. **delight** [dɪˈlaɪt] (n.) 愉快
6. **seize the opportunity** 把握機會
7. **collapse** [kəˈlæps] (v.) 攤倒
8. **enlarge** [ɪnˈlɑːrdʒ] (v.) 增大

Chapter Five

🎧 23

Advice From a Caterpillar

Alice wandered into a thick wood, looking for something to eat or drink. She saw a mushroom[1], about the same height as herself.

On tiptoe[2], she peeped[3] over the edge of the mushroom, and her eyes met those of a large caterpillar[4], resting on the top.

"Who are you?" Mr. Caterpillar inquired.

"Dear sir, I think I'd better not answer you. I'm sorry to disappoint you," Alice said.

---

1. **mushroom** [ˈmʌʃruːm] (n.) 蘑菇
2. **on tiptoe** 用腳尖著地
3. **peep** [piːp] (v.) 偷看
4. **caterpillar** [ˈkætərˌpɪlər] (n.) 毛毛蟲

24

"Why won't you tell me?" he asked.

"I think it has to do with the frequent changes in the size of my body. Being so many different sizes in a day is very confusing. Words and names just come out wrong," Alice explained politely.

"Show me," Mr. Caterpillar requested.

Alice tried to recite[1] an old poem:

1. **recite** [rɪˈsaɪt] (v.) 背誦
2. **gaze** [geɪz] (n.) 凝視
3. **argument** [ˈɑːrgjʊmənt] (n.) 爭論
4. **suspend** [səˈspend] (v.) 使中止
5. **corrosion** [kəˈroʊʒən] (n.) 腐蝕
6. **eyesight** [ˈaɪsaɪt] (n.) 視力
7. **guru** [ˈgʊruː] (n.) 上師
8. **supple** [ˈsʌpəl] (a.) 柔軟的
9. **impolite** [ˌɪmpəˈlaɪt] (a.) 粗魯的
10. **yoga** [ˈjoʊgə] (n.) 瑜伽
11. **weary** [ˈwɪri] (a.) 疲累的
12. **destruction** [dɪˈstrʌkʃən] (n.) 毀滅
13. **redemption** [rɪˈdempʃən] (n.) 救贖
14. **stake** [steɪk] (n.) 危險
15. **plight** [plaɪt] (n.) 困境
16. **despair** [dɪˈsper] (n.) 絕望
17. **gloom** [gluːm] (n.) 陰鬱

You are old and slow, teacher, yet your gaze[2]
is alert and intense.
I read very long essays in just one glance.
Arguments[3] keep away the need for corrective
lens,
For they suspend[4] the corrosion[5] of my eyesight[6].

You are old and fat, guru[7], yet your limbs are
loose and supple[8].
I bend in ways impolite[9] and informal.
Yoga[10] keeps my mind acute and body flexible,
Though I am not attraction to a woman's sight.

You are old and weary[11], traveler, yet your
heart is warm and open.
I drove my carriage through much
destruction[12].
Sympathy keeps my spirit tuned to
redemption[13],
To balance the stakes[14] of human plight[15].
I wipe away despair[16] and gloom[17], as I witness
history unfold.
My soul is a reserve of goodwill; my hopes are
firm and stable.

 Check Up

1. Why didn't Alice know how to introduce herself to Mr. Caterpillar?

25

"I'm afraid it is not right; some of the words have been altered[1], or perhaps your brain just faltered[2]," Mr. Caterpillar commented. "But who are you?" he asked again.

"I used to think I was Alice. However, I felt like Mabel when I was oversized. Consequently[3], I dare not say who I am, especially when I am this small." Alice tried her best to convey[4] to him her predicament[5].

"So, you see a reflection[6] of yourself in Mabel," he said.

"No, it is not quite like that," she said with uncertainty.

"So, you have multiple[7] identities," Mr. Caterpillar remarked[8] philosophically.

"You feel as if you had a twin inside you. It's not too bad. You'll always have a companion[9] with you in whatever venture you undertake[10] in your short life."

"Mabel! My twin! Inside me! Oh, never!" Alice cried in horror.

1. **alter** [ˈɔːltər] (v.) 改變
2. **falter** [ˈfɔːltər] (v.) 搖晃
3. **consequently** [ˈkɑːnsɪkwəntli] (adv.) 結果；因此
4. **convey** [kənˈveɪ] (v.) 傳達

"If it is simply about growing and shrinking, you'll get used to it once you learn how to control it."

"Here, one side makes you grow and the other makes you shrink," said Mr. Caterpillar.

"One side of what? And the other side of what?" asked Alice.

"Of the mushroom." With ease, Mr. Caterpillar flipped down from the mushroom, and then wiggled[11] away.

✓ Check Up **Choose the correct answer.**

T 2. It turned out that Alice and Mabel were twins.
F

3. What suggestion did Mr. Caterpillar give Alice?

_____

5. **predicament**
   [prɪˈdɪkəmənt] (n.) 困境
6. **reflection** [rɪˈflekʃən]
   (n.) 反射；倒影
7. **multiple** [ˈmʌltɪpəl] (a.)
   多重的；多樣的
8. **remark** [rɪˈmɑːrk]
   (v.) 談論；評論

9. **companion**
   [kəmˈpænjən] (n.) 同伴
10. **undertake** [ˌʌndərˈteɪk]
    (v.) 進行；從事
11. **wiggle** [ˈwɪgəl] (v.) 扭動

After the departure of Mr. Caterpillar, Alice tore off two pieces of the mushroom, one from either side. She took a bite of one piece to see what would happen.

Alice's neck stretched above the trees. She could see the outer rim[1] of the wood. "My goodness! My neck is as long as a snake! I can't see my feet! Oh, I can't see my hands!"

"A snake is here to steal my eggs and murder my future chicks!" a female pigeon shouted. "There should be a ban[2] on snakes here, on top of the trees."

"Mrs. Pigeon, I am not a snake. I don't even like raw[3] eggs," Alice shouted back at the bird.

✓ Check Up

4. Why did Mrs. Pigeon get so angry with Alice?

_____

1. **rim** [rɪm] (n.) 邊緣
2. **ban** [bæn] (n.) 禁止
3. **raw** [rɔː] (a.) 生的

"Eggs are eggs, be they raw or cooked. If you like eggs, then you are a snake," declared Mrs. Pigeon angrily.

"Evolution[1] is annoying. Why should I have wings when you have scales? I nested on telephone poles, and your type came. I nested on the ledges[2] of opera houses[3] and your type came."

1. **evolution** [ˌiːvəˈluːʃən] (n.) 進化
2. **ledge** [ledʒ] (n.) 壁架
3. **opera house** 歌劇院
4. **Mother Nature** 孕育萬物的大自然

"Mother Nature[4] is creative at the expense[5] of my offspring[6]. That is so unfair. There should be strict regulations[7] making it illegal for you to come here."

Then angry Mrs. Pigeon tried to peck[8] at Alice's eyes, but the bird was too slow. Alice had already taken a bite of the other piece of mushroom, and in an instant, she had shrunk back down into the wood.

"Now I can turn into any size I want to. I just need to find the way back to the lovely garden," she thought.

Alice's internal[9] organs felt twisted from the stretching and shrinking. However, she was pleased at being back to her normal size.

I'll rest a bit first. I am not on a tight schedule. I need to take some time to rest. Then, I will go and find that beautiful garden."

✓ Check Up   Choose the correct answer.

_____ 5. How did Alice shrink back to her normal size?
- A She ate the eggs of Mrs. Pigeon.
- B She took a bite of a mushroom.
- C She ate some grains on the farm.

5. **expense** [ɪk'spɛns] (n.) 代價
6. **offspring** ['ɔːfsprɪŋ] (n.) 後代
7. **regulation** [ˌrɛgjʊ'leɪʃən] (n.) 規章；條例
8. **peck** [pɛk] (v.) 啄
9. **internal** [ɪn'tɜːrnl] (a.) 內部的

Chapter Six

The Duchess and the Cheshire Cat

Instead of the garden, Alice soon found a big house. While she was wondering what to do next, a messenger[1] came running out of the wood and knocked at the door.

Curious to know what it was all about, Alice crept[2] a little way out of the wood to listen.

"For the Duchess[3] : an invitation from the Queen to play croquet[4]."

A butler[5] came out of the house and confronted[6] the Messenger. "Identification[7], please!"

1. **messenger** [ˈmesɪndʒər] (n.) 使者
2. **creep** [kriːp] (v.) 悄悄行進 (creep-crept-crept)
3. **duchess** [ˈdʌtʃɪs] (n.) 公爵夫人
4. **croquet** [kroʊˈkeɪ] (n.) 槌球
5. **butler** [ˈbʌtlər] (n.) 男管家
6. **confront** [kənˈfrʌnt] (v.) 迎面遇到
7. **identification** [aɪˌdentəfɪˈkeɪʃən] (n.) 身分證明

The Messenger flashed a badge[1] of some sort and said, "I am a messenger from the Queen of Hearts. I hope that your capacity[2] to relay[3] the message is reliable."

The Butler pulled a stern[4] face and uttered, "What? Your insolence[5] is disturbing[6]. I would like to remind you that I am your superior by rank."

"But I work for the Queen. We are not rivals[7] in rank. I await a declaration[8] on the intentions[9] of the Duchess regarding the game," the Messenger said in a solemn[10] voice.

"I expect the Duchess to evaluate[11] her desires and interests appropriately[12], so they will be in agreement with the Queen's wish."

1. **badge** [bædʒ] (n.) 徽章
2. **capacity** [kəˈpæsəti] (n.) 能力
3. **relay** [riːˈleɪ] (v.) 傳達
4. **stern** [stɜːrn] (a.) 嚴峻的
5. **insolence** [ˈɪnsələns] (n.) 傲慢
6. **disturbing** [dɪˈstɜːrbɪŋ] (a.) 煩擾討厭的

"And wait you shall," the Butler replied.

The Messenger and the Butler were competitors in a game of royal servant snobbishness[13] and queer speech. With their noses up in the air, they disregarded each other's presence and stood motionless.

Suddenly, the Butler ducked[14]. A saucepan[15] came flying out of the house and barely missed the Messenger. The Messenger ran away in horror, screaming, "Are you trying to murder me?"

"You bet," the Butler chased after the Messenger.

"I would never come again."

"The feeling is mutual[16]."

Alice could hear their angry voices in a distance.

✓ Check Up True or False

T
F
  1. Because he was a representative of the Queen of Hearts, the Messenger was in higher rank than the Butler.

T
F
  2. The Messenger ran away because he saw something horrible in the house.

7. **rival** [ˈraɪvəl] (n.) 對手
8. **declaration** [ˌdekləˈreɪʃən] (n.) 聲明
9. **intention** [ɪnˈtenʃən] (n.) 意圖
10. **solemn** [ˈsɑːləm] (a.) 嚴肅的
11. **evaluate** [ɪˈvæljueɪt] (v.) 評價
12. **appropriately** [əˈprouprɪˌeɪtlɪ] (adv.) 適當地

13. **snobbishness** [ˈsnɑːbɪʃnɪs] (n.) 勢利
14. **duck** [dʌk] (v.) 躲避
15. **saucepan** [ˈsɔːspæn] (n.) 平底鍋
16. **mutual** [ˈmjuːtʃuəl] (a.) 共同的；相互的

Alice went timidly[1] up to the door, opened it, and went in. The door led into a large kitchen. Inside the kitchen, a cook was cooking soup, and she was busy throwing all the different seasonings[2] she could find in the cupboard into a cauldron[3].

The Duchess sat nearby with a baby in her lap. A steady series[4] of sobs and howls[5] came from the baby. The smell of hot pepper filled the air.

Alice started to sneeze[6], and so did the Duchess. The baby alternated[7] between sneezes and howls.

"Who are you?" asked the Duchess, and then she snapped, "Shut up, you Pig!"

The Duchess said the last word with such sudden force that Alice almost jumped up with fear. But in an instant, she realized that it was addressed to the baby, not to her.

"Stop using your experimental[8] hot pepper, witch; it's giving the baby and me no peace," the Duchess shouted furiously[9] at the cook.

"I have devoted[10] my life to feeding you, and you call me a witch. Now that's gratitude[11]."

✓ Check Up True or False

T
F
    3. A witch was brewing a potion for the baby.

1. **timidly** [ˈtɪmɪdlɪ] (adv.) 膽怯地
2. **seasoning** [ˈsiːzənɪŋ] (n.) 調味料
3. **cauldron** [ˈkɔːldrən] (n.) 大汽鍋
4. **series** [ˈsɪriːz] (n.) 系列；連續
5. **howl** [haʊl] (n.) 嚎叫；怒吼
6. **sneeze** [sniːz] (v.) 打噴嚏

7. **alternate** [ˈɔːltərnɪt] (v.) 交替；輪流
8. **experimental** [ɪkˌsperɪˈmentl] (a.) 試驗性的
9. **furiously** [ˈfjuriəslɪ] (adv.) 猛烈地
10. **devote** [dɪˈvoʊt] (v.) 奉獻
11. **gratitude** [ˈgrætɪtuːd] (n.) 感恩

The cook began throwing utensils[1] at the Duchess and the baby. The baby was howling even louder than before. A large saucepan flew by the baby's nose and almost carried it off.

"What are you doing?" cried Alice. "Oh, there goes the baby's precious nose!"

Several dishes crashed at Alice's feet, and she jumped up and down in terror.

"I swear that this is a plot[2] to murder me. My funeral will come soon because of this witch. You take the baby, since you care for him. I must go and get ready to play croquet with the Queen."

---

1. **utensil** [juːˈtɛnsəl] (n.)
   器具；器皿

2. **plot** [plɑːt] (n.)
   密謀；陰謀

🎧 32

As the Duchess spoke, she turned and flung[1] the baby into Alice's arms. Out the doorway entrance ran the Duchess, followed by Alice carrying the baby.

"I can't leave it behind, because they are sure to kill it in a day or two," Alice said. The little baby grunted[2] in agreement. "Don't grunt," Alice admonished[3] it.

The baby grunted again, and Alice looked down at its face. To her shock, the baby had turned into a pig! Alice immediately set the little creature down, and it trotted[4] away into the woods.

1. **fling** [flɪŋ] (v.) 用力丟
   (fling-flung-flung)
2. **grunt** [grʌnt] (v.)
   豬發咕嚕聲
3. **admonish** [əd'mɑːnɪʃ] (v.)
   警告
4. **trot** [trɑːt] (v.)
   快步跑；快跑

Alice went into the forest and soon came across a Cheshire[1] cat resting on the bough[2] of a tree. Mr. Cheshire Cat was grinning[3] at Alice.

Alice approached him with suspicion. "Cats don't grin," she muttered[4] to herself. But he heard her, and said,

"Your knowledge of cats is quite inadequate[5]; we all grin. That is how our maker made us. We grin when we feel spiritual, like during funerals."

"Grinning at funerals is neither proper nor modest[6]," said Alice.

"Rubbish[7]!" he snapped. "Who says funerals are supposed to be modest or proper events?"

"Then, what is so spiritual[8] about now?" asked Alice.

"Very spiritual, young lady, because in whichever[9] direction you turn, you'll find madness," Mr. Cheshire Cat said prophetically[10].

"Why? Is there some virus that is spreading and making people mad?" she inquired.

1. **Cheshire** [baʊ] (n.)
   柴郡，英格蘭西北部
2. **bough** [baʊ] (n.) 樹幹
3. **grin** [grɪn] (v.) 露齒微笑
4. **mutter** [ˈmʌtər] (v.) 嘀咕

5. **inadequate** [ɪnˈædɪkwɪt]
   (a.) 不充分的；貧乏的
6. **modest** [ˈmɑːdɪst]
   (a.) 謙遜的；審慎的
7. **rubbish** [ˈrʌbɪʃ] (v.) 胡說

Alice thought about the hot pepper, the pig, and the madness in the kitchen of the Duchess. "Are you saying you're mad too?"

"Yes, we're all mad. Since you are here, you, too, must be mad. Being mad is the only way to be," explained Mr. Cat as he continued to grin.

"No, I disagree! I'm not mad, nor do I want to become mad!" exclaimed Alice. Then with a sweet smile on her face, she added, "Anyway, please tell me which way I should go."

"Well, now let me paint you a portrait[11] in words, of what you will find in all the directions," he replied.

"You're not being logical[12]. Portraits are created with brushes and paints of various colors, not with invisible words," complained Alice.

8. **spiritual** [ˈspɪrɪtʃuəl]
   (a.) 神聖的
9. **whichever** [wɪtʃˈevər]
   (pron.) 無論哪個
10. **prophetically** [prəˈfetɪkli]
    (adv.) 預言地
11. **portrait** [ˈpɔːrtrɪt] (n.) 畫像
12. **logical** [ˈlɑːdʒɪkəl] (a.) 邏輯的

✓ *Check Up* Choose the correct answer.

_____4. Which of the following is NOT true?
   Ⓐ Mr. Cheshire Cat could smile.
   Ⓑ Alice lost her mind because of Mr. Cheshire Cat.
   Ⓒ Alice did not think Mr. Cheshire Cat was being logical.

🎧 34

    Ignoring Alice's comment, Mr. Cat continued, "To the east, you'll find the Mr. March Hare[1]. To the west, you will find the Mr. Hatter. Both suffer from acute[2] depression[3] and should visit a mental-health clinic."

    "Mr. Hatter is filled with strange ideas, which causes an uncontrollable, even automatic, mouthing[4] of silly words."

    Alice became curious. "What kind of ideas?" she asked.

    "Very intellectual[5] ideas; they are all about the fabric[6] of the universe, the knit of space and time. Mr. Hatter has the ambition to become a metaphysician[7]. Of course, Mr. March Hare's madness comes from trying to figure out what Mr. Hatter means," Mr. Cat elaborated[8].

1. **hare** [her] (n.) 野兔
2. **acute** [əˈkjuːt] (a.) 嚴重的
3. **depression** [dɪˈprɛʃən] (n.) 沮喪；抑鬱
4. **mouth** [maʊθ] (v.) 言不由衷地重複說
5. **intellectual** [ˌɪntəˈlɛktʃuəl] (a.) 聰明的；知性的
6. **fabric** [ˈfæbrɪk] (n.) 織品；構造
7. **metaphysician** [ˌmɛtəfɪˈzɪʃən] (n.) 玄學家
8. **elaborate** [ɪˈlæbərət] (v.) 詳述

🎧 35

"Always figuring things out? Mr. March Hare sounds like an accountant," Alice said as she burst into[1] laughter.

"You laugh at sad facts. There is yet no remedy[2] for their illness. Nothing can eliminate[3] their disorders[4] except for a revolutionary[5] break through in psychiatry[6]. So, weigh your options[7] and choose your path carefully." Mr. Cat's grin grew larger.

"Well, since it is the merry month of May; maybe Mr. March Hare would not be too mad in the springtime. I'll go east," Alice decided.

"I'll see you later," Mr. Cheshire Cat said, and he slowly vanished, first the body, then the head, and finally the grin.

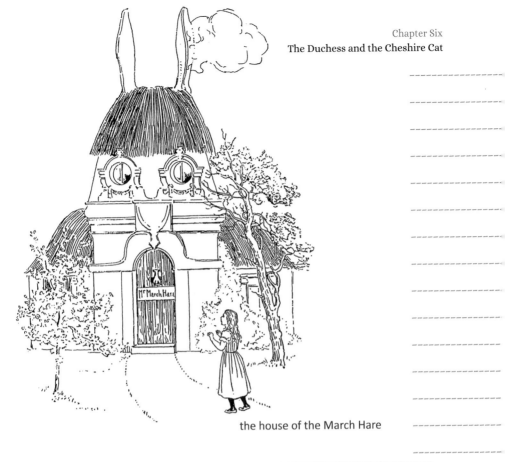

the house of the March Hare

Choose the correct answer.

_____5. Why did Alice think Mr. March Hare was like an accountant?

Ⓐ Because Mr. March Hare was good at math.

Ⓑ Because Mr. March Hare helped the Duchess to invest money.

Ⓒ Because Mr. March Hare was often trying to figure things out.

1. **burst into** 情緒的突然發作
2. **remedy** ['remɪdi] (n.) 治療
3. **eliminate** [ɪ'lɪmɪneɪt] (v.) 消除
4. **disorder** [dɪs'ɔːrdər] (n.) 失調
5. **revolutionary** [ˌrevə'luːʃəneri] (a.) 革命性的
6. **psychiatry** [səɪ'kaɪətri] (n.) 精神病治療
7. **option** ['ɑːpʃən] (n.) 選擇

Chapter Seven

🎧 36 A Mad Tea-Party

Alice came upon[1] an acre[2] of apple trees. Mr. Hatter, Mr. March Hare, and a male dormouse[3] were having tea at a large table in the shade of a particularly large apple tree.

"My mate, my dear friend, come; have some more tea. It's organic[4] and tastes superb[5]," Mr. Hatter said to Alice.

"I can't have more tea when I don't have any," said Alice while sitting down at the table.

✓ Check Up Choose the correct answer.

_____ 1. What's probably TRUE about Alice's response?
  Ⓐ Alice didn't like Mr. Hatter.
  Ⓑ Alice implied Mr. Hatter had made a grammar mistake when he invited her to have some tea.
  Ⓒ Alice hated tea.

---

1. **come upon** 偶然發現
2. **acre** [ˈeɪkər] (n.) 英畝;地產
3. **dormouse** [ˈdɔːrmaʊs] (n.) 睡鼠
4. **organic** [ɔːrˈɡænɪk] (a.) 有機的
5. **superb** [suˈpɜːrb] (a.) 一流的

🎧 37

"I give you my guarantee[1]; you can always have more, just not less." said Mr. Hatter while he balanced the teapot on top of a large pile of teacups[2].

Alice hesitated. The cloth on the table was stained[3] with preserves[4]. Ants were crawling in and out of the sugar bowls and jam bottles. Alice was sure that there were colonies[5] of ants living among the utensils[6].

Also, she was reluctant[7] to reach for the pot, because she was afraid the pile of teacups would collapse.

✓ Check Up | Choose the correct answer.

2. Choose the appropriate answer to fill in the blanks.

Shade of _____	Ⓐ ants	
Colony of _____	Ⓑ books	
Pile of _____	Ⓒ gray	
Pot of _____	Ⓓ tea	

1. **guarantee** [ˌɡærən'tiː] (v.) 保證
2. **teacup** ['tiːkʌp] (n.) 茶杯
3. **stain** [steɪn] (v.) 弄髒;沾汙
4. **preserve** [prɪ'zɜːrv] (n.) 蜜餞;果醬
5. **colony** ['kɑːləni] (n.) 群體
6. **utensil** [juː'tensəl] (n.) 器具
7. **reluctant** [rɪ'lʌktənt] (a.) 不情願的

"You have nothing urgent[1] to do, so take a break and quickly pour yourself some tea," Mr. Dormouse urged[2] Alice.

"I am not thirsty at all," Alice said. The three did not find Alice's response satisfactory. They all stared at her, and their staring at her prompted[3] Alice to reiterate[4], "I am not thirsty. I meant what I said."

"Well, say what you mean," very determined Mr. Dormouse pressed.

"I did. I said what I meant, and I meant what I said," Alice retorted[5] as she put on her most sweet and innocent smile to mask her true feelings.

1. **urgent** [ˈɜːrdʒənt]
   (a.) 緊急的
2. **urge** [ɜːrdʒ] (v.) 催促
3. **prompt** [prɑːmpt] (v.) 促使

4. **reiterate** [riˈɪtərɪt] (v.)
   反覆講
5. **retort** [rɪˈtɔːrt] (v.)
   回嘴；反駁

✓ *Check Up* **Choose the correct answer.**

_____3. What is the meaning of the word "reiterate"?
   Ⓐ To say or state again.
   Ⓑ To be very angry.
   Ⓒ To give an answer.

"Oh, did you?" snarled[6] Mr. Dormouse in a cynical[7] tone of voice. "Do you think 'I get what I like' and 'I like what I get' are identical in meaning?"

"You might just as well say that 'I see what I eat' is the same thing as 'I eat what I see,'" Mr. Hatter declared.

"Or, do you think 'I breathe when I sleep' can translate into 'I sleep when I breathe'?" Mr. March Hare added.

The three took delight in showing off their superiority[8] to Alice and making use of her for entertainment.

Alice could not think of any rebuttal[9]. Their table was dirty, their logic was sound, and their manners were bad.

"This orchard[10] is lovely," she said, trying to change the subject.

"Prime[11] real estate this is. I advertised to rent out a well of treacle[12], and it was taken up in no time," noted Mr. Hatter.

---

6. **snarl** [snɑːrl] (v.) 吼叫
7. **cynical** [ˈsɪnɪkəl] (a.) 憤世嫉俗的
8. **superiority** [suˌpɪriˈɔːrɪti] (n.) 優越
9. **rebuttal** [rɪˈbʌtəl] (n.) 反駁
10. **orchard** [ˈɔːrtʃəd] (n.) 果樹園
11. **prime** [praɪm] (a.) 最好的
12. **treacle** [ˈtriːkəl] (n.) 糖蜜

🎧 **39**

"Where is the well of treacle?" Alice asked.

"Just nearby, further down along that strip of cobblestones[1]," answered Mr. March Hare.

"People could sink in a well of treacle," commented Alice.

"No, they float very well. Pregnancy[2] can help you float like a boat. Elsie, Tillie, and Lacie were pregnant and naked when they leaped into the well. And of course, they were giggling[3]," Mr. Hatter explained to Alice.

Mr. Dormouse added, "Elsie, Tillie, and Lacie are artists and like to draw illustrations of things beginning with the letter 'm,' such as memory, minor, moonlight, mortgage[4], mother, muchness[5] . . ."

"You can't draw memory or muchness," Alice interrupted Mr. Dormouse.

"Did you ever talk to memory or muchness?" demanded[6] Mr. Dormouse.

"Of course not," Alice replied.

"Then you should say nothing!" Mr. Dormouse snapped.

✅ *Check Up* True or False

T
F 4. Alice thought it was impossible for someone to draw "memory" or "muchness."

---

1. **cobblestone** [ˈkɑːbəlstoʊn] (n.) 圓石；鵝卵石
2. **pregnancy** [ˈpregnənsi] (n.) 懷孕
3. **giggle** [ˈgɪgəl] (v.) 咯咯地笑
4. **mortgage** [ˈmɔːrgɪdʒ] (n.) 貸款
5. **muchness** [ˈmʌtʃnɪs] (n.) 許多
6. **demand** [dɪˈmænd] (v.) 查問

Alice was not happy with the rudeness of Mr. Dormouse. Obviously, these three individuals were not suitable for an extended[1] conversation.

The best time to leave them might be sooner rather than later. But in the meantime, she watched Mr. Hatter dipping[2] his timepiece[3] into his tea while he was eating a lime.

"Don't do that. If you do, soon your watch won't be able to keep time," warned Alice.

"Such hardware cannot make Time stay," argued Mr. Hatter. He clearly discounted[4] Alice's opinion, because he dipped his watch into the tea again.

"I'd say she lied. It is as plain as day[5]. Neither a tongue tied[6] watch sipping tea nor any natural phenomena[7], such as the tide on a roller coaster ride[8], can hold Time at bay," said Mr. March Hare with assurance[9].

Mr. Hatter burped[10] loudly, and then he said with a sigh, "Last year, the court commissioned[11] me to write a tune for a historic event, namely, the 25th anniversary of the Royal Wedding. I sang the tune at the celebration ceremony, and the Queen opined[12] that I was simply murdering time."

"Thus, my friendship with Time ended. He abandoned[13] me and went to sleep on top of a lime[14] tree. Ever since then, he won't do a thing I ask! It is always lime time and teatime."

"He? Who is he?" asked Alice.

"Time," replied Mr. Hatter. "We have no time to wash the tea sets, and we are exposed[15] to the afternoon sun all the time."

"So, this is a never-ending tea party. Right?" inquired[16] Alice.

1. **extended** [ɪkˈstendɪd] (a.) 延長的；擴大的
2. **dip** [dɪp] (v.) 浸；泡
3. **timepiece** [ˈtaɪmpiːs] (n.) 錶
4. **discount** [ˈdɪskaʊnt] (v.) 漠視某人的話
5. **as plain as day** 非常清楚
6. **tongue tied** 緘默的
7. **phenomena** [fɪˈnɑːmɪnɑ] (n.) 現象（單數phenomenon）
8. **on a roller coaster ride** 大幅高低起伏的狀況
9. **assurance** [əˈʃʊrəns] (n.) 保證
10. **burp** [bɜːrp] (v.) 打嗝
11. **commission** [kəˈmɪʃən] (v.) 任命；委託
12. **opine** [oʊˈpaɪn] (v.) 認為
13. **abandon** [əˈbændən] (v.) 放棄；拋棄
14. **lime** [laɪm] (n.) 萊姆；酸橙
15. **expose** [ɪkˈspoʊz] (v.) 暴露
16. **inquire** [ɪnˈkwaɪr] (v.) 詢問

"Yes. My advice, which is probably only worth less than a dime[1], is that you should never fool around[2] with Time." Mr. Hatter said in a thoughtful[3] tone.

"It is true that there is nothing new. I should have known that happy singing is a thought crime anytime the Queen is eating a lime."

BLANCHE McMANUS·

Then, Mr. Hatter, Mr. March Hare, and Mr. Dormouse dropped their heads onto their teacups and fell asleep. Alice took the opportunity to flee[4] the mad tea party.

✓ *Check Up* Choose the correct answer.

5. Fill in the blanks.

A murdering   B Muchness   C opportunity

1 _____ cannot be drawn.

2 Mr. Hatter was accused of _____ time when he sang to the Queen.

3 Alice fled when the _____ came.

---

1. **worth less than a dime** = not worth a dime 沒用處

2. **fool around** 遊手好閒

3. **thoughtful** [ˈθɔːtfəl] (a.) 深思的

4. **flee** [fliː] (v.) 逃走 (flee-fled-fled)

· Chapter Eight ·

🎧 42

The Queen's Croquet[1] Ground

Finally, Alice found the room with the little steel door. She took the key to the steel door, nibbled[2] at the mushroom, and shrank herself to the appropriate size.

Then she unlocked the door and walked into the beautiful garden, among the bright flower-beds and the cool fountains.

"Oh, how elegant it is!" Alice happily breathed the fragrant[3] air. Two odd men who looked like playing cards were painting the roses with concentration[4].

1. **croquet** [ˈkrəʊkeɪ] (n.) 槌球
2. **nibble** [ˈnɪbəl] (v.) 一點一點地咬
3. **fragrant** [ˈfreɪgrənt] (a.) 芳香的
4. **concentration** [ˌkɑːnsənˈtreɪʃən] (n.) 專心

43

"The roses from here to the left are yours." With a strange tone, Mr. Five of Clubs[1] assigned Mr. Three of Clubs the task. "I'll have your head if they are not painted red by sundown[2]."

"Don't mock[3] the queen's accent! Be content that you still have your head," said Mr. Three of Clubs.

One by one, white roses turned red under the neat and refined[4] brush strokes[5] of the two cards.

"This job is dull[6] and disgraceful, too. I am a scholar, a biology graduate from King's College. I look ridiculous wielding[7] a paintbrush[8]," said Mr. Three of Clubs. "How long can roses last without oxygen[9]?"

"I am a physicist[10]; I know nothing about the chemistry[11] of photosynthesis[12]. You're the biologist here," replied Mr. Five of Clubs.

1. **club** [klʌb]
   (n.)（紙牌的）梅花

2. **sundown** [ˈsʌndaʊn]
   (n.) 日落

3. **mock** [mɑːk]
   (v.) 模仿；嘲弄

4. **refined** [rɪˈfaɪnd]
   (a.) 精緻的

5. **stroke** [stroʊk] (n.) 筆觸

6. **dull** [dʌl] (a.) 乏味的

7. **wield** [wiːld] (v.) 揮舞著

8. **paintbrush** [ˈpeɪntbrʌʃ]
   (n.) 油漆刷

9. **oxygen** [ˈɑːksɪdʒən]
   (n.) 氧氣

10. **physicist** [ˈfɪzɪsɪst]
    (n.) 物理學家

11. **chemistry** [ˈkemɪstri] (n.)
    化學；化學性質；化學作用

12. **photosynthesis**
    [ˌfoʊtəˈsɪnθɪsɪs] (n.)
    光合作用

"But I'm a zoologist, not a botanist. Anyway, I don't think oxygen is an ingredient[13] in the production[14] of chlorophyll[15]," said Mr. Three of Clubs.

Suddenly, they panicked and the dialog halted[16]. They threw themselves flat on the damp[17] garden soil and called out, "Hail[18]!"

✅ Check Up Choose the correct answer.

T
F
_____ 1. One card thought that the Queen had a strange accent.

_____ 2. Which of the following occupations is not mentioned here?
Ⓐ zoologist   Ⓑ physicist
Ⓒ biologist   Ⓓ chemist

---

13. **ingredient** [ɪnˈgriːdiənt]
    (n.) 原料；要素；成分
14. **production** [prəˈdʌkʃən]
    (n.) 生產；製造
15. **chlorophyll** [ˈklɔːfɪl]
    (n.) 葉綠素

16. **halt** [hɔːlt] (v.) 停止
17. **damp** [dæmp] (a.) 潮濕的
18. **hail** [heɪl] (v.) 歡呼；打招呼

44

Along came the royal suite[1] of Hearts. Last of all in the grand parade were the King and Queen of Hearts!

"Who are you?" the Queen asked Alice.

"I am Alice, Your Majesty," Alice introduced herself as she curtseyed. The Queen was quite pleased.

"Alice, meet the diplomatic[2] delegate[3] from the influential[4] suite of Hearts," demanded the Queen. Mr. Knave[5] of Hearts nodded at Alice.

"Come and play croquet with us," the Queen commanded Alice. Alice joined the procession[6].

The royal party turned and headed toward a field beside a canal[7]. At the field, a page[8] equipped Alice with a flamingo[9] for a mallet[10].

The flamingo was quite a load for Alice to carry. The Playing Cards folded themselves over like hoops[11]. The balls were live hedgehogs[12].

"I have never seen such a curious croquet ground in my life," Alice said to herself.

✅ *Check Up* Choose the correct answer.

_____ 3. What is NOT included in playing a croquet game?
Ⓐ a flamingo   Ⓑ a hedgehog   Ⓒ a basketball

---

1. **suite** [swiːt] (n.) 隨從
2. **diplomatic** [ˌdɪpləˈmætɪk] (a.) 外交的
3. **delegate** [ˈdelɪgət] (n.) 代表
4. **influential** [ˌɪnfluˈenʃəl] (a.) 有影響的；有權勢的

5. **knave** [neɪv] (n.)
（紙牌中的）傑克（jack）

6. **procession** [prə'seʃən] (n.)
行列；隊伍

7. **canal** [kə'næl] (n.) 運河

8. **page** [peɪdʒ] (n.) 侍從

9. **flamingo** [flə'mɪŋɡoʊ] (n.)
紅鶴

10. **mallet** ['mælɪt] (n.) 木槌

11. **hoop** [huːp] (n.) 球門

12. **hedgehog** ['hedʒhɑːɡ] (n.)
刺蝟

45

Either the hedgehogs were forever running away, or they fainted whenever they were hit.

Alice felt it was a sin to hit one live animal with another, and she just could not stretch out her flamingo's neck to use it as a mallet.

The Queen screamed at the top of her lungs[1] at anyone who had difficulty handling the animals.

A strange apparition[2] appeared in mid-air. It emitted[3] a multicolored[4] radiation[5].

As it grew, Alice frowned[6]. Her instinct[7] told her that she would soon be able to recognize this fluttering[8] ball of colored lights.

✔ Check Up **True or False**

T
F
4. Alice had difficulty in playing with a real animal.

---

1. **at the top of one's lungs** 聲嘶力竭
2. **apparition** [ˌæpəˈrɪʃən] (n.) 幻影；幽靈
3. **emit** [ɪˈmɪt] (v.) 放射
4. **multicolored** [ˈmʌltiˌkʌlərd] (a.) 彩色的
5. **radiation** [ˌreɪdiˈeɪʃən] (n.) 發光
6. **frown** [ˈfraʊn] (v.) 皺眉
7. **instinct** [ˈɪnstɪŋkt] (n.) 直覺
8. **fluttering** [ˈflʌtərɪŋ] (a.) 飄動的

🎧 46

Players began to gather underneath[1] the fluttering ball. The glow grew larger and stayed in the air, as if it was going to maintain a permanent[2] residence[3] in the sky.

The ball of lights turned into a ball of fur. The ball was a partial[4] appearance of Mr. Cheshire Cat. His appearance was partial because only his head was visible.

"Off with his head," the Queen shouted. "Anyone that interferes[5] with the game must be beheaded[6]."

"But there's no body for the head to be detached[7] from. You can't behead someone with such a disadvantage[8]," Mr. Knave of Hearts argued.

"You can always further[9] disadvantage the disadvantaged. As long as he has a head, then he can be beheaded," explained the King, who found no merit[10] in Mr. Knave of Hearts' argument.

"The cat belongs to the Duchess. Perhaps you'd better talk to the Duchess first." Alice tried to rescue Mr. Cheshire Cat by diverting[11] their attention.

"But the Duchess is in prison," the King replied.

"Well, get her anyway!" the Queen ordered. Alice accepted the Queen's order and saw it as a chance to flee the game.

1. **underneath** [ˌʌndərˈniːθ] (prep.) 在……之下
2. **permanent** [ˈpɜːrmənənt] (a.) 永遠的；固定性的
3. **residence** [ˈrezɪdəns] (n.) 居住；留駐
4. **partial** [ˈpɑːrʃəl] (a.) 部分的
5. **interfere** [ˌɪntərˈfɪr] (v.) 妨礙
6. **behead** [bɪˈhed] (v.) 把……砍頭
7. **detach** [dɪˈtætʃ] (v.) 使分開
8. **disadvantage** [ˌdɪsədˈvæntɪdʒ] [前] (n.) 不利條件 [後] (v.) 使處於不利地位
9. **further** [ˈfɜːrðər] (adv.) 進一步地
10. **merit** [ˈmerɪt] (n.) 價值；優點
11. **divert** [dɪˈvɜːrt] (v.) 使轉向

✔ *Check Up* Choose the correct answer.

_____ 5. Mr. Cheshire Cat first appeared in the air above the croquet field as _____.
 (A) a croquet ball   (B) lightning   (C) a ball of lights

"Pity my master, who is imprisoned[1]," Mr. Cheshire Cat spoke loudly, and gasps[2] broke forth[3] from all the surprised onlookers[4].

"My head will be quite secure[5]." As Mr. Cat spoke, his eyes sparkled[6] like crystals.

"No one can kill me. I can only die by suicide, which, hopefully, will never be, because I am not mad like you." Mr. Cat broke into a wide grin and disappeared.

✓ Check Up

6. When did Alice get away from the croquet game?

_____

1. **imprison** [ɪmˈprɪzən] (v.) 監禁
2. **gasp** [gæsp] (n.) 倒抽一口氣
3. **break forth** 突發

4. **onlooker** [ˈɑːnˌlʊkər] (n.) 觀眾
5. **secure** [sɪˈkjur] (a.) 安全的
6. **sparkle** [ˈspɑːrkəl] (v.) 發光

Chapter Nine

🎧 48

The Mock¹ Turtle's Story

As she escaped the mad game, Alice ran into the Duchess. "I thought you were in prison!" Alice exclaimed.

The Duchess replied, "My crime is nothing serious. The King is sometimes kind and will pardon those who were ordered to be beheaded. You'll see."

Then she looked at Alice's flamingo. "I hope your flamingo does not bite like mustard². I have proposed a new rule for my kitchen: No pepper! Well, no mustard, too."

✔ Check Up Choose the correct answer.

_____1. What did the Duchess mean when she said "I have proposed a new rule for my kitchen"?

Ⓐ The Duchess wanted to build a new kitchen.

Ⓑ The Duchess wanted to avoid using some ingredients.

Ⓒ The Duchess was going to write her own recipe.

---

1. **mock** [mɑːk] (a.) 假的
2. **mustard** ['mʌstərd] (n.) 芥末。因芥末吃起來味道辛辣，引申為某人脾氣不好。

Alice suspected that although the Duchess could tell the difference between pepper and mustard, she could not distinguish[1] between a plant and a bird.

The Duchess rambled on[2]: "I will implement[3] this rule in my kitchen like a constitution. An orderly[4] kitchen is my new ideal. I won't need any kitchen staff because to rule with a new rule is a very economical way to rule. I will dismiss[5] the cook. She is old and should retire anyway . . . "

The Duchess dominated[6] the conversation and expanded[7] her ideas into a very long speech.

The Duchess' speech was a meaningless formation of words to Alice. "Perhaps the Duchess should write out her words to assist her audience. I could understand her better if I could read what she's saying," Alice thought.

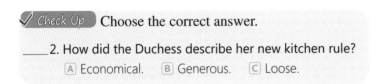

Check Up Choose the correct answer.

_____ 2. How did the Duchess describe her new kitchen rule?

Ⓐ Economical.　　Ⓑ Generous.　　Ⓒ Loose.

1. **distinguish** [dɪˈstɪŋgwɪʃ] (v.) 區別
2. **ramble on** 漫談下去
3. **implement** [ˈɪmplɪment] (v.) 實施
4. **orderly** [ˈɔːrdərli] (a.) 有條理的
5. **dismiss** [dɪsˈmɪs] (v.) 開除
6. **dominate** [ˈdɑːməneɪt] (v.) 支配；主導
7. **expand** [ɪkˈspænd] (v.) 擴展

Suddenly, the Queen appeared from nowhere[1]. With her arms folded in front of her chest, she gave the Duchess a warning: "Leave or I'll chop[2] off your head!"

The Duchess ran away quickly. The Queen turned to Alice and gave her a warning, too.

"Return to the Championship[3] Croquet Game, or you'll lose your head!" Alice followed the Queen back to the game.

All the players panicked at the Queen's arrival. Soon she imprisoned everyone except for Alice, the King, and Mr. Knave of Hearts. Obviously, she wanted badly to become a croquet champion.

Valuable lives were endangered[4] because of the Queen's ambition. All the prisoners begged for mercy[5].

Luckily, this grave[6] situation was only temporary and was resolved[7] very soon. The King, who sometimes had high moral values, was keen[8] to release the prisoners. He pardoned[9] everyone as soon as the Queen turned away.

Check Up

3. After the Queen put many players in prison, who were left to play the croquet game with her?

_____

1. **nowhere** [ˈnoʊwer] (n.)
   不知什麼地方
2. **chop** [tʃɑːp] (v.) 砍
3. **championship**
   [ˈtʃæmpiənʃɪp] (n.) 錦標賽
4. **endangered** [ɪnˈdeɪndʒərd]
   (a.) 即將絕種的
5. **mercy** [ˈmɜːrsi] (n.) 仁慈
6. **grave** [greɪv]
   (a.) 嚴重的；嚴峻的
7. **resolve** [rɪˈzɑːlv] (v.) 解決
8. **keen** [kiːn] (a.) 熱衷的
9. **pardon** [ˈpɑːrdn] (v.) 赦免

🎧 51

For reasons unknown[1] to Alice, the Queen brought Alice to a gryphon[2]. Mr. Gryphon was a strange creature with the head of an eagle and the body of a lion.

Mr. Gryphon opened his eyes with a pop and stared at Alice. The Queen ordered Mr. Gryphon to take Alice to Mr. Mock Turtle, who lived in isolation[3], far away from the royal grounds.

Alice cast away[4] her flamingo, because the bird was a heavy load to carry. Mr. Gryphon took Alice through a gap between two boulders[5] and found the turtle near a cliff[6].

Mr. Mock Turtle possessed[7] the skill of storytelling and had the reputation[8] of being the saddest person ever known.

"I'm sad because I want to go home. But why do you look so sad?" asked Alice.

"Oh, dear," Mr. Mock Turtle began his story. "Once upon a time, I was a real turtle. I went with my classmates to a school in the sea. Some great masters taught us lots of things. My first teacher was an old turtle, but we called him Mr. Tortoise[9]."

"Why did you call him Mr. Tortoise if he was a real turtle?" Alice asked.

"We called him Mr. Tortoise because he taught us slowly. Teaching slowly was his profession," the sad turtle replied.

1. **unknown** [ʌnˈnoʊn] (a.) 未知的
2. **gryphon** [ˈɡrɪfən] (n.) 半獅半鷲的怪獸，是希臘神話中的怪獸，也是牛津大學三一學院的徽章。
3. **isolation** [ˌaɪsəˈleɪʃən] (n.) 隔離；孤立
4. **cast away** 丟掉
5. **boulder** [ˈboʊldər] (n.) 巨石
6. **cliff** [klɪf] (n.) 懸崖峭壁
7. **possess** [pəˈzes] (v.) 擁有
8. **reputation** [ˌrepjʊˈteɪʃən] (n.) 名聲
9. **tortoise** [ˈtɔːrtəs] (n.) 陸龜；烏龜

✅ Check Up **True or False**

T
F
4. Mr. Mock Turtle enjoyed being the happiest person in the world.

52

Mr. Gryphon uttered[1] some unrecognizable[2] words as a protest against Alice's question.

"Be quiet, Mr. Gryphon!" Mr. Mock Turtle snapped, and then continued his story. "In those days, conventional[3] schools mostly taught only music and French. At our very exclusive[4] school, we learned washing."

"But Mr. Mock Turtle, you live in the sea; washing has no application[5] there," Alice challenged Mr. Mock Turtle. "Moreover, you don't need clothing; you have a shell. What do you have to wash?"

"Shells are a turtle's clothes. I have spare shells to wear and dirty shells to wash. Just like you with your clothes," Mr. Mock Turtle defended himself.

"We had the best of education, and we learned the different branches of arithmetic, you know, Ambition, Distraction, Uglification[6], and Derision[7]," noted Mr. Gryphon, who was eager to get some respect for all the difficult subjects he had once studied.

"How can you calculate[8] with uglification? Do you mean multiplication instead?" Alice asked as she tried to interpret[9].

"You are very dull. Uglification is the opposite of beautification," Mr. Gryphon explained impatiently.

1. **utter** ['ʌtər] (v.) 出聲；說
2. **unrecognizable** [ʌn'rekəgnaɪzəbəl] (a.) 無法辨認的
3. **conventional** [kən'venʃənəl] (a.) 傳統式的
4. **exclusive** [ɪk'skluːsɪv] (a.) 獨有的

5. **application** [ˌæplɪ'keɪʃən] (n.) 運用；施用
6. **uglification** [ˌʌgləfɪ'keɪʃən] (n.) 醜化
7. **derision** [dɪ'rɪʒən] (n.) 嘲笑
8. **calculate** ['kælkjʊleɪt] (v.) 計算
9. **interpret** [ɪn'tɜːrprɪt] (v.) 解釋；理解

✓ Check Up Choose the correct answer.

_____ 5. What was NOT the reason Alice challenged Mr. Mock Turtle?

A Mr. Mock Turtle lived in the sea.

B Mr. Mock Turtle needed no clothing, because he had a shell.

C Mr. Mock Turtle didn't know how to apply water.

113

53

"How can you calculate using beauty?" asked Alice.

"Shame on you! Stop interfering! Cease[1] these impolite and meaningless inquiries[2]!" Mr. Gryphon exclaimed as his nasty[3] facial expression accused[4] Alice of being a rude troublemaker[5].

Mr. Mock Turtle continued his story, "The dramatic crab taught us the Classics of Laughing and Grieving. He was gifted with toughness and crabbiness[6]. He also ran a very strict classroom."

"That crab was a tough critic[7] of contemporary[8] literature, especially when he analyzed romantic novels," Mr. Gryphon added.

Mr. Mock Turtle continued in a sad voice, "On the first day of school, we had ten hours of lessons, the second day nine hours, the third day eight hours . . . "

✓ Check Up   Choose the correct answer.

_____ 6. Why was Mr. Gryphon angry with Alice?
   A He thought Alice was too silly to understand what "beautification" was.
   B He thought Alice was asking some impolite questions.
   C He thought Alice had insulted his master.

"Why did you reduce the length of the lessons by one hour every day?" Alice interrupted.

"Lessons are lessons because they lessen[9]!" Mr. Gryphon explained very impatiently as he glared[10] at her again.

Alice thought, at this rate of reduction[11], there would be no time left to reduce on the 11th day of school. She silently concluded that the 11th day had to be a holiday.

1. **cease** [siːs] (v.) 停止
2. **inquiry** [ɪnˈkwaɪri] (n.) 詢問
3. **nasty** [ˈnæsti] (a.) 惡意的
4. **accuse** [əˈkjuːz] (v.) 指控
5. **troublemaker** [ˈtrʌbəlˌmeɪkər] (n.) 麻煩製造者
6. **crabbiness** [ˈkræbinəs] (n.) 易怒；好抱怨
7. **critic** [ˈkrɪtɪk] (n.) 評論家
8. **contemporary** [kənˈtempəreri] (a.) 當代的
9. **lessen** [ˈlesən] (v.) 變少
10. **glare** [gler] (v.) 怒視
11. **reduction** [rɪˈdʌkʃən] (n.) 減少

Chapter Ten

The Lobster Quadrille[1]

"Let's educate her about our games," Mr. Gryphon suggested.

"Oh, I am looking forward to the day we can dance the magnificent Lobster Quadrille again," the sad turtle said with a groan[2].

"I know how to dance the Minuet[3]," Alice said excitedly.

"Oh, the two types of dances are different in minute[4] and subtle[5] ways," Mr. Mock Turtle explained. "I even composed a verse for the future return of the lobsters.

But since the lobsters are regarded as outlaws[6], no publisher would correspond[7] with me to discuss its publication. There is a ban on any talk of the lobsters' long march away from here."

1. **quadrille** [kwɑːˈdrɪl] (n.) 方舞舞曲（需要四對舞伴的舞蹈）
2. **groan** [groʊn] (n.) 呻吟聲
3. **Minuet** [ˌmɪnjuˈet] (n.) 小步舞曲
4. **minute** [maɪˈnuːt] (a.) 微小的
5. **subtle** [ˈsʌtəl] (a.) 微妙的
6. **outlaw** [ˈaʊtlɔː] (n.) 罪犯；放逐者
7. **correspond** [ˌkɔːrɪˈspɑːnd] (v.) 通信

55

"Do you have a shortage[1] of lobsters?" asked Alice.

"They all left. None have remained," Mr. Mock Turtle almost cried.

"This is their native habitat[2]. Nonetheless[3], they left," Mr. Gryphon said sadly. "The Queen is a reformed capitalist[4], a very aggressive one. She released a new economic policy and enforced[5] it with rigor[6]. "

"She quickly gathered a lot of money. Lobsters that didn't comply with[7] her demands were given capital[8] punishment. Rounding[9] up lobsters and making them into mechanical toys was a prominent[10] feature of the Queen's new policy. "

"Most of the lobsters perceived[11] the danger. To avoid the Queen's crazy economic policy and to keep their heads attached to their bodies, the lobsters simply marched away."

"Her obsession[12] with getting the economy to work for her benefit became a central element in her psychological[13] complex."

1. **shortage** [ˈʃɔːrtɪdʒ] (n.) 不足
2. **habitat** [ˈhæbɪtæt] (n.) 棲息地
3. **nonetheless** [ˌnʌnðəˈles] (adv.) 但是；仍然

4. **capitalist** [ˈkæpɪtəlɪst] (n.) 資本家
5. **enforce** [ɪnˈfɔːrs] (v.) 執行
6. **rigor** [ˈrɪɡər] (n.) 嚴厲；嚴格
7. **comply with** 遵守
8. **capital** [ˈkæpɪtl] (a.) 處死刑的

9. **round** [raʊnd] (v.) 圍捕
10. **prominent** [ˈprɑːmɪnənt]
   (a.) 顯著的
11. **perceive** [pərˈsiːv] (v.) 察覺

12. **obsession** [əbˈseʃən]
   (n.) 著迷
13. **psychological**
   [ˌsaɪkəˈlɑːdʒɪkəl] (a.) 心理的

✓ Check Up   Choose the correct answer.

_____1. Who made the lobsters leave their native habitat?
   Ⓐ The Queen.
   Ⓑ Mr. Mock Turtle.
   Ⓒ Nobody made them leave. Those that chose to stay lost their heads.

56

Mr. Mock Turtle began his verse:

"By imperial[1] decree[2],
Our dear Queen's capitalism[3] was here."
A queer[4] new economy
Rolled over every enemy.

A rebel lobster was born.
Oh, he was fearless.
They called him Rebel[5] Leader Titum,

Lobsters pledged[6] their loyalty
To Titum the Revolutionary.
The whole gang[7] went to sea
And shouted, "Learn how to return!"

How quickly collapsed the Queen's
economy.
The triumphant[8] lobsters understood
When Rebel Leader Titum said, "Try to be
good."

The sad turtle let out a long sigh and continued, "That big departure of the lobsters was such a tragedy[9]. I don't think I will ever dance the Lobster Quadrille again in my lifetime."

Mr. Gryphon wanted to be positive, so he said, "Rumors have it that a new Quadrille is all the rage[10] on other continents and the lobsters go everywhere these days."

Alice was also tired of listening to the sad story of the lobsters, so she suggested cheerfully, "Let's dance!"

"Yes, let's dance! A turtle should be the commander[11]," Mr. Gryphon announced.

 Check Up

2. Who is Titum?

_____

 3. After the lobsters left, Mr. Mock Turtle thought he would never dance the Lobster Quadrille again.

1. **imperial** [ɪmˈpɪriəl] (a.) 專橫的
2. **decree** [dɪˈkriː] (n.) 命令
3. **capitalism** [ˈkæpɪtəlɪzəm] (n.) 資本主義
4. **queer** [kwɪr] (n.) 古怪的
5. **rebel** [ˈrebəl] (n.) 反抗者
6. **pledge** [pledʒ] (v.) 許諾

7. **gang** [gæn] (n.) 一群
8. **triumphant** [traɪˈʌmfənt] (a.) 勝利的
9. **tragedy** [ˈtrædʒɪdi] (n.) 悲劇
10. **all the rage** 風行一時
11. **commander** [kəˈmændər] (n.) 指揮官

121

Mr. Turtle objected, "But I don't have a porpoise[1]. I need a porpoise in order to call out the moves."

"Don't you mean 'purpose'?" Alice asked.

"I mean a commander without a porpoise will only cause chaos[2]. No one will have a clue as to what the commander's calls are," explained the sad turtle.

"I can help you. Come on," Mr. Gryphon begged.

Mr. Mock Turtle turned to Alice and declared, "We can only give you a hint of what this amazing dance is like."

"First, all the creatures line up on the shore except those evolved[3] from the classification of bivalves[4]." Mr. Turtle led Alice and Mr. Gryphon to form a line.

Mr. Gryphon explained, "Then, the commander calls out 'Heehum' and the line echoes[5] his call."

"Heehum!" Mr. Mock Turtle cried.

"Heehum!" Alice and Mr. Gryphon echoed.

"Then catch a lobster and squeeze[6] it. Then twist its tail. Then march forward two steps," commanded Mr. Mock Turtle.

Alice and Mr. Gryphon acted out[7] the commands.

 Check Up   True of False

T
F
4. Mr. Mock Turtle cried out loud because nobody was listening to his command.

1. **porpoise** [ˈpɔːrpəs] (n.) 海豚
2. **chaos** [ˈkeɪɑːs] (n.) 混亂
3. **evolve** [ɪˈvɑːlv] (v.) 進化
4. **bivalve** [ˈbaɪvælv] (n.) 雙殼貝
5. **echo** [ˈekoʊ] (v.) 回應
6. **squeeze** [skwiːz] (v.) 擠；榨
7. **act out** 把……付諸行動

"Then throw the lobster into the sea and wait for it to shoot out from the water like a missile[1]. Then swim there and catch it again. Then flip[2] and drift[3] back to the shore," ordered Mr. Mock Turtle.

Alice and the Gryphon acted out the described actions.

Mr. Mock Turtle continued, "Then exchange lobsters when the commander calls out 'Nasty Pincers[4].' Ready? 'Nasty Pincers!'"

At his command, Alice and Mr. Gryphon exchanged invisible[5] crustaceans[6] with ease and grace.

"Then we go into the second figure," huffed[7] Mr. Gryphon. He was getting short of breath.

 Check Up

5. How do you know that the dance was very tiring to Alice?

_____

"This dance is really a tremendous workout[8]," said Alice. She was also huffing[9] and puffing[10].

"The objective is to work all your muscles during the entire dance," Mr. Mock Turtle explained, "and the amount of workout should be equivalent[11] to a croquet game."

"The trial of Mr. Knave of Hearts is beginning," someone shouted in the distance.

"Let's go!" Mr. Gryphon shouted, and Alice hurried to follow him to the imperial courthouse[12].

1. **missile** [ˈmɪsəl] (n.) 飛彈
2. **flip** [flɪp] (v.) 翻轉
3. **drift** [drɪft] (v.) 漂流
4. **pincer** [ˈpɪnsər] (n.) 螯；鉗子
5. **invisible** [ɪnˈvɪzɪbəl] (n.) 隱形的
6. **crustacean** [krʌˈsteɪʃən] (n.) 甲殼類
7. **huff** [hʌf] (v.) 深呼吸

8. **workout** [ˈwɜːrkaʊt] (n.) 身體鍛鍊
9. **huff and puff** 上氣不接下氣
10. **puff** [pʌf] (v.) 喘氣
11. **equivalent** [ɪˈkwɪvələnt] (a.) 相等的
12. **courthouse** [ˈkɔːrthaʊs] (n.) 法院

· Chapter Eleven ·

🎧59 Who Stole the Tarts[1]?

The trial[2] took place in the palace. With an artificial[3] expression on her face, the Queen sat on her throne[4] in front of a sculpture of herself dressed as Lady Justice[5, 6].

In the center was a table with a tray of tarts on it. All the creatures of this wonderland were gathered nearby. Bill the Lizard and the whole gang from the Caucus Race were the jurors[7].

Alice could not get close to the tasty-looking tarts, because the jury box[8] was in the way. The jury box was a barrier between her and the sweets.

1. **tart** [tɑːrt] (n.) 餡餅
2. **trial** ['traɪəl] (n.) 審判
3. **artificial** [ˌɑːrtɪ'fɪʃəl] (a.) 不自然的
4. **throne** [θroʊn] (n.) 王座
5. **justice** ['dʒʌstɪs] (n.) 法官
6. **Lady Justice** 正義女神，古羅馬之神，雙手分別持天平和寶劍，緊閉雙眼或眼睛蒙著布條
7. **juror** ['dʒʊrər] (n.) 陪審團
8. **jury box** 陪審員席

The King entered, and a burst of applause[1] rose. Mr. White Rabbit, acting as the Court Herald[2], called out, "Silence in the court!" He held up a piece of paper and read, "The Knave of Hearts stole some of the Queen's tarts."

"What is your verdict[3]?" the King asked the jury[4].

"No, no, no, Your Majesty[5]! No hurry for the verdict! At least there should be an oral cross-examination[6] of the witnesses; otherwise, our court will have to face some bad publicity[7]. Appearances must be maintained. Writers of journals are present," Mr. Rabbit said. "Call the Duchess' cook."

Alice's Adventures in Wonderland

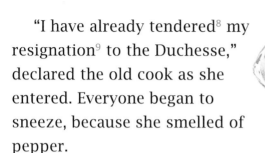

"I have already tendered[8] my resignation[9] to the Duchesse," declared the old cook as she entered. Everyone began to sneeze, because she smelled of pepper.

The King sneezed hard, and then he finally managed to ask, "What do you know about the stolen tarts?"

Alice looked at the tarts again and was puzzled[10]. "But the tarts are right there!" she cried out.

"I did not ask you, young lady! Cook, answer me now," demanded the King.

1. **applause** [əˈplɔːz] (n.) 拍手；鼓掌
2. **herald** [ˈherəld] (n.) 傳令官
3. **verdict** [ˈvɜrdɪkt] (n.) 裁定
4. **jury** [ˈdʒuri] (n.) 陪審團；評審委員會
5. **Majesty** [ˈmædʒəsti] (n.) 陛下
6. **cross-examination** 交叉詰問
7. **publicity** [pəˈblɪsəti] (n.) 名聲
8. **tender** [ˈtendər] (v.) （正式）提出
9. **resignation** [ˌrezɪgˈneɪʃən] (n.) 辭職；辭呈
10. **puzzled** [ˈpʌzəld] (a.) 困惑的

"I know nothing. Tarts do not capture my attention. Soup-making is my craft[1], not bakery," the cook answered.

"What were you doing when the tarts were stolen?" the King continued.

"I was shopping. I was excited because the spring catalog of herbs had arrived. I am now setting up my own workshop[2], where I can perform surgery[3] on lizards. I'll also run a nursery[4] for rhubarbs[5]." Bill the Lizard shivered[6] as the ex-cook for the Duchess explained her plans.

"Fine. You can leave now." The King dismissed[7] the ex-cook, and then he commanded, "Call the next witness!"

"Call Mr. Hatter!" Mr. White Rabbit shouted.

"Why is that Time-Killer still alive?" the Queen roared in anger.

✔ **Check Up** Choose the correct answer.

_____ 1. What was the Duchess' ex-cook interested in?
- Ⓐ Stealing tarts.
- Ⓑ Playing with lizards.
- Ⓒ Making soup.
- Ⓓ Making bakery.

---

1. **craft** [kræft] (n.) 手藝
2. **workshop** [ˈwɜːrkʃɑːp] (n.) 工坊
3. **surgery** [ˈsɜːrdʒəri] (n.) 外科手術
4. **nursery** [ˈnɜːrsəri] (n.) 苗圃

"One crime at a time, please," the King intervened[8].

"I . . . I am but a poor . . . poor folk of l . . . l . . . l . . . low learning, and know nothing of t . . . t . . . tarts . . . tarts." Mr. Hatter managed to upset the Queen with his slow speech.

"You are a very poor speaker. You need speech therapy[9]. You stutter[10] quite a bit. Now, you may go." The King dismissed Mr. Hatter.

Mr. Hatter secretly grabbed three tarts as he went on his way. He said in a whisper to Alice, "Three tarts for . . . tea, but none for thee."

"I took the liberty[11] of searching the personal belongings[12] of Mr. Knave of Hearts and found this plain piece of paper in his toilet kit," declared Mr. White Rabbit, who seemed to act as a detective, police officer, counsel[13], and Court Herald[14] in the court.

✓ Check Up Choose the correct answer.
_____ 2. Who seemed to have multiple functions in court?
　Ⓐ Mr. Hatter.　　　　Ⓑ The King.
　Ⓒ The Queen.　　　　Ⓓ Mr. White Rabbit.

5. **rhubarb** [ˈruːbɑːrb] (n.) 大黃（一種植物）

6. **shiver** [ˈʃɪvər] (v.) 發抖

7. **dismiss** [dɪsˈmɪs] (v.) 讓……離開

8. **intervene** [ˌɪntərˈviːn] (v.) 插入

9. **therapy** [ˈθerəpi] (n.) 治療

10. **stutter** [ˈstʌtər] (v.) 結巴地說話

11. **liberty** [ˈlɪbərti] (n.) 許可

12. **belongings** [bɪˈlɔːŋɪŋz] (n.) 財產；物品

13. **counsel** [ˈkaʊnsəl] (n.) 律師；辯護人

14. **herald** [ˈherəld] (n.) 傳令官

"Paper can be used for a note or letter. Be quiet! Let me process this new development for a minute . . . " The King fell silent, and the air was electrifying[1].

"Ah-ha, that paper strengthens my case against that thief of tarts," the Queen spoke with passion. "Not signing your letters is equivalent[2] to masking[3] your identity which proves mischief[4]. And the lack of handwriting is a perfect fit."

"But the paper is blank," cried the Knave of Hearts.

The Queen screamed impatiently, "Who is the intended receiver of this note? Who is your correspondent[5]? The subject matter of this trial is no small matter. How could anyone gain admission to the royal kitchen without my permission? There must be a plot, some evil machinery[6] to bring about the collapse of our economy. It is the cruel plot of an obvious spy to

✓ Check Up Choose the correct answer.

T 3. The Queen thought that Mr. Knave of Hearts had
F   tried to steal all the sweets.

_____ 4. What was the reason the Queen thought for the tarts
        being stolen?
   A To ruin the country's economy.
   B To create evil machinery.
   C To increase the nation's wealth.

steal all our sweets and rocket our national deficit[7] far into the sky!"

Poor Mr. Knave of Hearts tried to explain, "But I'm not a . . ."

"Where is the headquarters of your operation[8]?" The Queen was furious. She was breathing heavily which caused her breasts to weave[9] back and forth as they heaved[10] up and down. "Your guilt is obvious. No more joint economic ventures[11] with you. Refusal[12] to admit your guilt[13] is useless."

"That's it," the King told the jury, "and before I can relieve[14] you of your duty, you must fulfill[15] your responsibility concerning this individual's terrible wickedness . . . "

1. **electrifying** [ɪˈlektrɪfaɪɪŋ] (a.) 非常激動人心的
2. **equivalent** [ɪˈkwɪvələnt] (a.) 等同的
3. **mask** [mæsk] (v.) 掩飾
4. **mischief** [ˈmɪstʃɪf] (n.) 損害
5. **correspondent** [ˌkɔːrɪˈspɑːndənt] (n.) 通信者
6. **machinery** [məˈʃiːnəri] (n.) （政府等的）機構
7. **deficit** [ˈdefɪsɪt] (n.) 赤字
8. **operation** [ˌɑːpəˈreɪʃən] (n.) 操作；經營
9. **weave** [wiːv] (v.) 搖晃
10. **heave** [hiːv] (v.) 鼓起；起伏
11. **joint venture** 合資企業
12. **refusal** [rɪˈfjuːzəl] (n.) 拒絕
13. **guilt** [gɪlt] (n.) 罪行
14. **relieve** [rɪˈliːv] (v.) 解除職務
15. **fulfill** [fʊlˈfɪl] (v.) 履行

🎧 63 "Sentence[1] that spy right now!" shouted the Queen, "and there is no other possible sentence in the running[2] besides beheading."

"No! How can you sentence somebody before listening to a verdict[3]?" Alice shouted.

"Why not? We, being true democrats[4], practice not only the separation of the church and the state but also the separation of verdict and sentence. One is not the prerequisite[5] of the other. It is the ideal of any democracy," explained the Queen, with her usual air of absolute[6] authority[7].

"Such a procedure[8] is quite efficient in that it leaves no margin[9] for error and no room for negotiation[10]. Any sentence I arrange for will always fit the magnitude[11] of the crime. The verdict is always 'guilty as charged.' Everyone knows that."

Alice was getting pretty bored with this strange trial. She turned to Mr. Gryphon, who was sitting beside her, and said, "They haven't proven anything. There is no real evidence[12], hence[13] a verdict of innocent[14] should be the result."

As Alice spoke, she began to grow bigger. "Why? I didn't eat a piece of mushroom, and I didn't drink anything either," Alice wondered.

✓ *Check Up* True of False

T
F
5. The Queen thought that the jury's verdict should be innocent as charged.

1. **sentence** ['sɛntəns] (v.) 判決
2. **running** ['rʌnɪŋ] (n.) 運轉
3. **verdict** ['vɜ:rdɪkt] (n.)
   （陪審團的）裁決
4. **democrat** ['dɛməkræt] (n.)
   民主主義者
5. **prerequisite** [pri:'rɛkwɪzɪt] (a.)
   不可缺的
6. **absolute** ['æbsəlu:t] (a.) 絕對的
7. **authority** [ə'θɔ:rɪti] (n.) 權力
8. **procedure** [prə'si:dʒər] (n.) 程序
9. **margin** ['mɑ:rdʒɪn] (n.) 餘裕
10. **negotiation** [nɪˌgouʃi'eɪʃən] (n.)
    協商
11. **magnitude** ['mægnɪtu:d] (n.)
    大小；強度
12. **evidence** ['ɛvɪdəns] (n.) 證據
13. **hence** [hɛns] (adv.) 〔書〕因此
14. **innocent** ['ɪnəsənt] (a.) 無罪的

135

Chapter Twelve

🎧 64

Alice's Evidence

"There is one more witness[1], Your Majesty." Mr. Rabbit reminded the King, and then he called out, "The court calls Alice."

Alice stood up and knocked over the jury box.

Everyone was greatly shocked. "What on earth[2] transformed that girl into a giant?" exclaimed the Queen.

"Rule 47, a person over a mile tall cannot be a witness. It is the oldest rule," the King said.

"If it is the oldest, it should be Rule 1!" Alice said. "Besides, I am not a mile tall."

"It is not necessary for the oldest to be the first. I am a lawyer and I founded this justice system, so I know full well what the oldest rule is," the King argued.

---

1. **witness** [ˈwɪtnɪs] (n.) 證人   2. **what on earth** 到底是什麼

"Then you should also know that it is a universal rule to decide the sentence only after a verdict of guilty is given by the jury," declared Alice. She felt it was her duty to protest against the procedure of the court.

"Contempt[1] of court[2]! For the unity of the Four Suites, off with this female monster's head," the Queen ordered.

By this time, Alice realized that she was taller and bigger than anyone in this court. She said bravely, "I'm not afraid of you. You're nothing but a pack of cards."

This made the Cards furious[3], and they all began to take action. Immediately, an explosion blasted[4] out.

Flames of orange and pink shot forward. The Cards went flying at Alice with their sharp edges . . . .

✓ Check Up Choose the correct answer.

_____1. What did Alice protest about the trial?
   Ⓐ The oldest rule should the first.
   Ⓑ The justice system should not have been founded by the King.
   Ⓒ The court should have heard a verdict of guilty before trying to sentence Mr. Knave of Hearts.

1. **contempt** [kənˈtempt] (n.) 蔑視
2. **contempt of court** 藐視法庭
3. **furious** [ˈfjuriəs] (a.) 狂怒的
4. **blast** [blæst] (v.) 爆炸

Alice woke up on the grassy slope by the riverbank. Her sister was reading nearby.

"What a land of fantasy my nap[1] transported me to!" Alice exclaimed[2].

"You go to the cinema too often," her sister said with a smile.

"Still, what a dream it was!" Alice exclaimed again. "It was a very different era in my dream, and yet, also very familiar. I know it was just a piece of fiction, but it feels so real. How exciting!"

She recounted[3] the details of her dream to her sister as she brushed away the fallen leaves from her dress. Beside her, lizards lazed and absorbed[4] the last rays of the setting sun, which looked like a glowing[5] pink and orange disk.

1. **nap** [næp] (n.) 午睡；小睡
2. **exclaim** [ɪkˈskleɪm] (v.) 驚叫
3. **recount** [rɪˈkaʊnt] (v.) 詳細敘述
4. **absorb** [əbˈsɔːrb] (v.) 吸收
5. **glowing** [ˈgloʊɪŋ] (a.) 明亮的
6. **vivid** [ˈvɪvɪd] (a.) 鮮明的
7. **adjust** [əˈdʒʌst] (v.) 調整
8. **leaflet** [ˈliːflɪt] (n.) 傳單
9. **volunteer** [ˌvɑːlənˈtɪr] (n.) 志工

The dream was so vivid[6]. It took some time for Alice to adjust[7] to reality. After the sunset, Alice, with a plan in her mind, followed her sister back home. Alice wanted to write stories.

The next Saturday afternoon, Alice and her older sister were at their local church.

A leaflet[8] announcing a search for volunteers[9] to work at the day care center was posted on the notice board by the entrance.

Alice was too young to meet the requirements for applicants. She was not eligible[10] for registration as a volunteer day care worker, but the church officials did welcome her to be registered[11] as an informal helper.

10. **eligible** [ˈelɪdʒɪbəl] (a.)
有資格的

11. **register** [ˈredʒɪstər] (v.)
登記

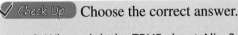 **Check Up** Choose the correct answer.

_____ 2. What might be TRUE about Alice?
    Ⓐ She had dreams only about dogs and frogs.
    Ⓑ She was a movie lover.
    Ⓒ She wrote fiction.

Ⓣ 3. Alice was qualified to apply for the day care center's
Ⓕ   volunteer.

67

The sisters left the church with smiles on their faces. Alice, holding the registration receipt in her hands, felt as if a new adventure was about to begin.

She began dancing along the sidewalk. Immediately, all the sounds and colors around her began to mix and weave. An ethereal[1] concert seemed to ring out. The overhead electrical power line[2] hummed a message.

Were the electrical wires transmitting[3] the latest news about all the inhabitants[4] of Wonderland?

An array of fantastic images and characters began to form in Alice's imagination. Soon, she would have other tales of mysterious[5] journeys to tell.

---

1. **ethereal** [ɪ'θɪrɪəl] (a.) 天上的；非人間的
2. **power line** 電線
3. **transmit** [træns'mɪt] (v.) 傳送
4. **inhabitant** [ɪn'hæbɪtənt] (n.) 居民
5. **mysterious** [mɪ'stɪrɪəs] (a.) 神祕的；不可思議的

68

Her older sister watched Alice dance and thought about her little sister's amazing stories. She believed Alice would grow up to become a great writer, a designer of engaging[1] tales of wonder.

Yes, Alice would, in some way, always be a bright and delightful[2] little girl who was full of interesting stories to stimulate[3] the imagination of curious readers around the world.

✓ **Check Up** Choose the correct answer.

_____ 4. Alice's sister thought that Alice would become _____.
  Ⓐ A clothing designer
  Ⓑ A bookstore owner
  Ⓒ A great writer

1. **engaging** [ɪnˈɡeɪdʒɪŋ] (a.) 迷人的；有魅力的
2. **delightful** [dɪˈlaɪtfəl] (a.) 令人愉快的
3. **stimulate** [ˈstɪmjʊleɪt] (v.) 刺激

Translation

[第一章] 墜入兔子洞

p. 10-11 懶洋洋的春天，只聽見蟋蟀唧唧鳴唱。愛麗絲和姊姊在河岸邊休息；姊姊埋首閱讀雜誌中一篇介紹印度詩人的文章。

愛麗絲想用雛菊編項圈給她的貓黛娜。她請姊姊幫忙，卻被斷然拒絕：「不要！」

姊姊平常也是這樣，如果在看書時打擾她，她就會對你發脾氣。於是，愛麗絲只好一個人四處閒晃。

忽然間，一隻穿著短外套的公白兔映入愛麗絲的眼簾。

「我的耳朵要掉了！我的鬍鬚要裂開了！我遲到了！」白兔先生看著懷錶驚慌失措叫著。

「看得懂時間的兔子！真是稀奇啊。」愛麗絲喃喃自語。她覺得一隻聰明絕頂的兔子，絕對會是個很棒的故事，她可以好好向朋友炫耀一番。

愛麗絲大叫：「哦，白兔先生！」

但白兔不理會她，只見他哭喊著：「哦，天啊，我遲到了！」

禁不住自己的好奇心，愛麗絲跟在白兔後面追了出去。

p. 12 白兔在大樹底下倏然停住腳步，他撥開草叢，露出了一個兔子洞。他向愛麗絲招了招手，以眼神示意她跟著來。

為了展現自己的勇敢，愛麗絲二話不說跟著白兔先生進了洞穴。兔子洞陡直，她感覺自己彷彿摔進了一座深井中。

在下墜中途，愛麗絲看到一張大英帝國的巨型地圖，她想像自己穿越層層土壤，到達另一端的澳洲。身為遙遠國度的旅客，她認為有機會教導澳洲人合宜的禮儀，會是她的榮幸。

她往下掉的途中，還一邊嘗試練習屈膝禮，但想要在墜落同時成功屈膝實在很困難。

p. 14 「萬一我最後掉到一個蝙蝠洞該怎麼辦？」愛麗絲感到很恐慌。「我記得有很多傳聞說，澳洲部分地區有很多類似的洞穴，天啊，真希望黛娜現在在我身邊。」

不論是白天晚上，愛麗絲總愛把黛娜帶到房間，這樣就能確保老鼠不會偷偷溜進來。愛麗絲對「蝙蝠是在學飛的老鼠」這個看法深信不疑。如果黛娜在的話，即使掉進了當地的蝙蝠洞，她也不會感到恐懼。

「不過黛娜喜歡待在家裡。」愛麗絲心想：「為了她好，她還是不要跟著我一起來好了。」

p. 16-17 最後，愛麗絲跌落在一片細枝和枯葉堆上，它們靜靜地鋪排在原地，迎接每個從兔子洞掉落的人。

愛麗絲看到白兔先生急忙向前趕路，便追了上去。不久，她跑進了一間滿是門的房裡，房間以維多利亞風格所建。白兔先生已失去蹤影，而所有門都上了鎖。

愛麗絲在房間桌上發現一把金鑰匙，旁邊還有一個寫著「喝我」的瓶子。鑰匙能打開一扇窄小的鐵門，但愛麗絲根本鑽不過去。鐵門通往了一座美麗花園。

不經思索，愛麗絲將鐵門關上鎖好，把鑰匙歸回桌上，她打開瓶口。

愛麗絲聞聞味道，確認裡面裝的不是酒，因為小孩子不能喝酒。瓶裡沒有傳出酒味，愛麗絲很好奇它嚐起來是什麼味道。

「只喝一小口應該死不了吧。」愛麗絲打開瓶子啜飲了一些，接著又喝了一點。它喝起來很順口，有著酸櫻桃的味道。愛麗絲便一口氣喝光了整瓶。

令她想不到的是，她的身體竟然開始縮小，原來酒瓶裡面裝了會縮小人身體的液體。

p. 18–19 「可惜姊姊沒看到我變小的精采過程，彷彿今天這驚奇之事，不過日常生活的平凡事罷了。」看著自己的身體越變越小，愛麗絲興奮地做出了這番評語。

「萬一我就這樣一直變小，就消失了呢？那不就完蛋了！」她忽然擔心了起來。

愛麗絲沒讓恐懼打倒意志，她開始替自己禱告。突然，她身體不再縮小了。

她現在只有幾吋高，正好能穿過鐵門進入那美麗的花園。

不過難題來了，她現在太小拿不到桌上的鑰匙。

「白兔先生呢？有沒有誰可以幫幫我？」她無助地呼喊。

此時，她發現桌底有個小玻璃盒子。愛麗絲打開盒子，裡頭有塊小蛋糕，表面用葡萄乾排著「吃我」兩個字。她想也不想就把蛋糕吃下肚。

[第二章] 淚池

p. 20 吃下蛋糕後，愛麗絲的身體開始變大，才一下子，她的頭就頂到了天花板，身高足足有九呎高！愛麗絲輕鬆地拿起放在桌上的鑰匙，但她現在巨大的身軀，根本穿不過那窄門。她感到很沮喪，挨著身體躺了下來。

就在這時，她聽見外頭傳來一陣急促的腳步聲，探頭張望，看見白兔先生跑了回來，手裡拿著一把扇子。

愛麗絲的內心很焦急，一心想要向任何人求助。

「救命啊，白兔先生！請幫幫我！」愛麗絲想要引起白兔的注意，讓他停下腳步，但是白兔丟掉手中的大扇子，快步跑過她身邊。

p. 22-23 愛麗絲想撿起掉落的扇子，不過被自己龐大的手臂擋住。現在哪怕是一個微小的動作，都需花上她更大的專注與力氣。愛麗絲覺得自己像極了一個肢體殘障者，雙腳和雙手的距離簡直是相隔太遠了。

「如果我繼續長大，我就得買新鞋，再把鞋子寄去給我的腳。」'愛麗絲覺得這想法太荒謬了。

「我在作夢嗎？我意識清醒嗎？我還是原來那個愛麗絲嗎？」她感覺自己的腦袋昏沉沉的，好像變得跟她朋友梅寶一樣頭腦渾沌。

「我才不是梅寶，我可是有憑為證！我比她精明多了，我知道在英格蘭領的薪水是新加坡元，而在法國領的是日幣。」

「等等！這樣不對，各行各業的人都會被搞混的。他們所用的支票或是銀行帳戶，都用外國語來寫，而且付款金額也會出錯。」

「不過，也許有少部分人會很高興能使用新加坡幣和日幣。商人可以藉機抬高石油、小麥和稻穀的價格。」

「因為貨幣系統出現混亂，說不定有人會把銅當成黃金，而把銀當作白金，錢財大起大落，因為沒人知道物品的真正價格。」

「天啊，我變成梅寶了！我真要是她，我會沒有爸爸，沒有錢，在學校品性不端，也不懂什麼是經濟。哦，我的天啊！我怎麼會變那麼笨？為什麼每件事都那麼不真實呢？」

p. 24-25 愛麗絲對自己的反省，反而讓她更沮喪。擔心的感覺使她忍不住哭泣，從她臉頰滑落的斗大淚珠，像瀑布般傾瀉而下。方才白兔先生掉落的扇子浮了起來，愛麗絲伸手拾起扇子替自己搧風，因為她忽然覺得很熱。

「這裡有沒有人可以給我一些指引啊？誰是這裡的房東？我的小腦袋瓜沒辦法控制這麼大的身體。」

愛麗絲的眼淚流個不停，「我需要顧問，需要有人幫我釐清混亂，告訴我我的真實身分是誰。」

愛麗絲自言自語，搧著風，「真希望姊姊現在在這裡給我一些指導，她一定有證據可以證明我不是梅寶，我不想一個人孤零零地待在這裡！」

轉眼間，愛麗絲發現自己開始縮小，馬上就回到原本的大小了，原來用扇子搧風會把身體變小。她急忙丟掉扇子，免得自己會變得太小到消失無影。

她心想：「天啊！我的身體可能會因此消失不見呢，還好我逃過一劫，真是好險！」

p. 26–27 一陣波浪突然襲來，愛麗絲摔進了水深淹及下巴的鹹水裡，這是她剛剛變到九呎高時流的淚水，眼看她就要淹死在自己的淚池中了！

「早知道我就不要一直哭了！」愛麗絲說，她在水中奮力游著，希望找到方法脫身。

「喂！」有人高聲呼叫著她。愛麗絲看見遠方有個輪廓像是老鼠的東西在游泳。大部分的蝙蝠擅長飛行，而一般老鼠則是游泳健將。

即使只是隻老鼠，只要牠有一流的泳技，都能大大增加她活命的機會。淹死絕對不是個好選擇，所以愛麗絲決心游到那隻老鼠身邊。

「抓好我身上的毛，爬到我背上來。」老鼠先生說。

愛麗絲把手指伸進老鼠的毛中，順勢爬了上去。

愛麗絲感到十分疲憊，很高興老鼠先生願意當她的小船。

p. 28–29 「妳年紀輕輕，可是游泳的姿勢很漂亮，讓我印象深刻。在大水急流中，這可是一流的技術啊。」老鼠先生表示。

「謝謝你的誇獎！我只是拼命游，因為我怕淹死。」愛麗絲說。

老鼠先生信心十足地強調：「我們就快靠岸了。」

愛麗絲回應：「真的嗎？可我沒看見前面有陸地啊？」

「妳現在是在質疑我的判斷嗎？」老鼠生氣地厲聲問。

「不是。」愛麗絲低聲回答。在奮力游泳後，她尚未緩過氣來，不想惹毛老鼠先生。

「請妳說話大聲點。我已經老了，耳朵不靈光，連自己的聲音也聽不太清楚。」老鼠大聲地說，「妳怕活老鼠嗎？」

「通常我會怕，但是黛娜不會讓老鼠一類的動物靠近我。」愛麗絲告訴老鼠先生。

「誰是黛娜？」老鼠問。

「她是我的貓。」愛麗絲回答。

「我最討厭貓了！牠們是卑鄙的生物。」老鼠先生憤怒地說。

「我不這樣認為。黛娜很可愛……」

「少跟我說什麼可愛的貓！」老鼠先生大聲斥責。

他靜默了幾秒後問：「要是妳是我，妳還會喜歡貓嗎？」

「應該不會吧。在這個諾大的宇宙裡，我跟你都是那麼微不足道。」

p. 30–31 「如果黛娜現在在這裡，她可能根本認不出我來，甚至還會追著我跑，對我做出更可怕的事。」愛麗絲的回答滿是同情與哀傷。

不過話鋒一轉，她興奮地說：「你真會游泳！我們應該很快就會到岸了！」愛麗絲想用熱烈的讚美閃避剛剛的話題。

很明顯地，不管是怎樣的老鼠或蝙蝠，都對會追捕牠們的貓沒有任何好感。現在談論黛娜的聰明與可愛，似乎愚蠢又沒意義，對她現在的處境一點幫助都沒有。

「說得仔細點，我們距離岸邊還有十二多呎遠。」老鼠先生說。他開始計算每呎的距離給愛麗絲聽。

[第三章] 會議式賽跑與長篇故事

p. 32 愛麗絲注意到岸邊有些騷動。等到她的雙眼適應了黑暗，她看出了有一排奇怪的生物，河堤上聚集了長得很古怪的鳥和其他動物，每隻全身濕透又發冷，看來非常不舒服。

「加入我們吧。」渡渡鳥說，她的聲音高亢彷彿在唱歌一般。愛麗絲和老鼠先生欣然接受了邀請。

大家互相依偎取暖，現場一片寂靜。每個人盡量不隨便亂動，好節省自己的體力。

p. 34–35 愛發號施令的老鼠先生首先打破沉默，他提議用一個方法把大家弄乾。他的聲音變得很低沉地說：

「歷史本來就乾巴巴的，來講一個古英國的故事，鐵定能除去大家身上的濕氣。」老鼠以歷史學家的口吻，敘述起一篇長篇歷史故事。

「羅馬教皇支持威廉進攻英吉利海峽以北民族的目標，此舉讓征服者威廉認為，他的舉措獲得了上帝——也就是奇蹟與奧義操控者的支持。當他帶兵一舉攻下倫敦，他發現必須要……」

「發現什麼？」鴨子太太問，她的問題惹惱了老鼠先生。

「就是『發現』。」他生氣地回答。「妳不知道『發現』什麼嗎？」老鼠咆哮著，鴨子太太不敢再多問一句。

「我們還是濕漉漉的。」鴨子太太小聲抗議。

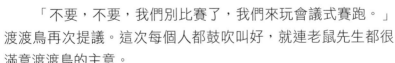

老鼠嚴肅地宣布：「好吧，我辭去將大家弄乾的這個職位。」接著便轉身回座。

「我們做些運動來把自己弄乾吧。」渡渡鳥說。

「好主意！我們組成兩隊吧。」鸚鵡提議。

「不要，不要，我們別比賽了，我們來玩會議式賽跑。」渡渡鳥再次提議。這次每個人都鼓吹叫好，就連老鼠先生都很滿意渡渡鳥的主意。

p. 36–37 他們彼此繞成圓圈，在地上畫出了奇怪的形狀當跑道。

「可是跑道只有一條呢！」愛麗絲覺得它看起來很怪。

鴨子太太解釋：「用上帝給妳的頭腦，有創意一點好嗎！妳應該能找到人生中的道路吧，所以只要用點想像力，就能找到妳自己的跑道。」

「但是我……」

「我們是不是該禁止她參賽啊？」不等愛麗絲說完，鴨子太太便打岔。

大家紛紛詢問渡渡鳥小姐的意見，最後她做出了聲明：「不行，每個人都要參加比賽，她會找到自己的跑道的。」

接著，渡渡鳥說出了一條表示「結束的相反」的線索，也就是比賽正式「開始」。

聽到指令，所有參賽者撞成一團，這場比賽自然變成了一場鬧劇。

當大家累到再也跑不動，也沒力氣撞別人時，渡渡鳥小姐便宣布：「比賽結束，每個人都是贏家。現在誰手上有獎品？」大家都沒有，除了愛麗絲之外。

p. 38 「我這裡有一些糖果。」愛麗絲從口袋拿出一盒糖，幸好所有的糖果都沒弄濕。她將糖果分送給每個人，不過糖果似乎不太夠，每個人都拿到一塊，只有愛麗絲自己沒有。

「她也要有獎品。」鴨子太太表示。

渡渡鳥小姐便問愛麗絲：「妳口袋還有別的東西嗎？」

「還有一個頂針。」愛麗絲回答。

「拿過來給我。」渡渡鳥小姐說著，便拿走了愛麗絲的頂針。

渡渡鳥細細瞧了頂針，接著宣布：「雖然這小小的金屬蓋子是從妳口袋拿出來的，但它並不屬於妳。所以妳參賽的獎品就是這枚精緻的頂針了。」渡渡鳥小姐如同在念詩般誦讀著。

p. 40–41 在場的動物們高聲歡呼。愛麗絲覺得這整件事荒謬至極，不過還是深深一鞠躬，將頂針收回自己的口袋。

無論如何，她很感激渡渡鳥小姐提出的賽跑意見。大家能盡情享受遊戲，分享糖果，而且現在每個人的身子都已經乾了。

「好，讓我來跟大家說個故事吧。」老鼠先生認真地說。

「又是故事？」鴨子太太問。

「大家已經弄乾了。」鸚鵡先生回應。

老鼠先生不理會他們的話，開始講起故事來了：

「這是一個長長的悲傷故事……」

「好吧，你的尾巴是很長，但是尾巴怎麼會悲傷呢？」愛麗絲問。她全被搞糊塗了。（譯註：老鼠說的 tale 是指「故事」，但是愛麗絲聽成了 tail「尾巴」。）

「妳胡說八道羞辱我！」老鼠憤憤不平地大喊：「再見！」他便頭也不回地走了。

「拜託你回來把故事說完吧。」愛麗絲追在老鼠身後，但是老鼠毫不領情。

「要是黛娜在就好了，她可以幫我把老鼠先生追回來。」愛麗絲嘆了一口氣。

「誰是黛娜？」渡渡鳥小姐發問。

「黛娜是我養的貓。」愛麗絲解釋：「她最會抓老鼠了，而且啊，她也很擅長追捕蝙蝠和小鳥喔！」

p. 42–43 「黛娜會吃小鳥嗎？」渡渡鳥小姐問，她又驚又怕。

愛麗絲立刻就後悔剛剛脫口而出的那些話，「哦，抱歉，我忘記妳是鳥了。」

「看吧，孩子。」渡渡鳥小姐向一旁的小螃蟹尖聲說：「這小女孩的心腸真壞，我們該回家了。」

鴨子太太對鴨寶貝們說：「來吧，孩子們，睡覺時間到了。」

老喜鵲也說：「我真的得回家了，晚上的空氣對我的喉嚨不大好。」

一個一個，動物們都找藉口回去了。沒多久，又留下愛麗絲一個人了。她孤獨地喃喃自語：「早知道我就不要說黛娜的事了。這裡，不管這裡究竟是哪裡，似乎沒有人喜歡貓。我可憐的黛娜！」

過了一會兒，愛麗絲又聽到一陣腳步聲，她急忙張望，希望是老鼠先生回來要把剛才的故事說完。

[第四章] 白兔先生與小比爾

p. 44　四下靜謐無聲，只有一陣腳步聲劃破了沉默。接著只聽見一個熟悉的聲音從寂靜中響起，原來是白兔先生，他口中不停喃喃說些什麼。

「我的扇子呢？我遲到了，公爵夫人會把我處死的！天啊，她現在掌控我的生死大權……」

當白兔看見愛麗絲，他興奮地大喊：「喔，瑪莉安，妳在這裡做什麼？盡好妳僕人的本分，回家替我把扇子拿來，快點！」

p. 46-47　「這是我的榮幸，先生。」愛麗絲毫不考慮就接受了自己的新身分，成為白兔先生的女僕。

她跑向白兔所指的方向，心中滿是驕傲：「我能隨機應變，因為我有顆靈活的頭腦。」

不過她隨即發現，自己進入了狹長走道，越深入，走道就變得越小，像根管子，她得爬著前進。最後，她從管中爬了出來，來到一座小山丘頂的農場，裡頭的穀物成熟可收成了。

牛隻在房屋邊吃草，房子亮銅色門牌刻著「白兔先生」。愛麗絲敲門，沒有人回應，便開門進去。

她看到房內擺設了皮革家具，不過沒看到什麼扇子，倒是發現了一個瓶子。瓶子和之前不同，並沒有寫上「喝我」的標籤。

「不論我喝了或吃下什麼，都會有好玩的事發生。」她對自己說：「我來看看喝下這瓶會怎麼變，希望可以讓我變長大，身體那麼小真是煩死人了。」愛麗絲拔去瓶口塞子喝下去。

　　果真被她猜中了！才喝不到一半，愛麗絲的身體開始放大，頭又頂到了白兔先生家的天花板。

　　她急忙放下瓶子，想要在這壓迫空間中調整好手臂和雙腳的位置。她只好把一隻手伸出窗外，一隻腳則是擠上了煙囪。

p. 48–49 「瑪莉安！瑪莉安！快把扇子拿來！」愛麗絲聽到白兔先生在窗外大叫。

　　「比爾，你這蜥蜴在哪裡？」

　　「白兔先生，找我嗎？」有人用破文法回應。

　　「那應該就是蜥蜴比爾吧。」愛麗絲心想。

　　「在窗戶上的是什麼？」白兔先生問。

　　「是一隻手臂，活生生的手，很明顯地。」比爾回道。

　　「它不該出現在這裡，拿走它。」白兔命令。

　　出於本能，愛麗絲揮動手臂，比爾還沒來得及靠近她，他們兩人就被揮了出去，在空中翻滾，摔到遠方。

　　比爾哀嚎著：「我到了天堂嗎？」他明顯摔得不輕。

　　「還早呢，」白兔先生回答，努力從地上爬起來。他拍拍身上灰塵，再度面對大手說：「我們得燒了這棟房子。」

　　「你們要再靠近我，我就叫我的貓黛娜去抓你們。」愛麗絲大叫。她的威脅讓當場氣氛陷入死寂。

　　「在這裡，講理和邏輯根本就行不通。」愛麗絲心想：「最有效的方法，就是用比他們大的動物來嚇唬，或許恐懼是統治人心理與行為的最終法則。」

p. 50–51 忽然間，愛麗絲聽到白兔先生大喊：「瞄準……發射！」一塊塊小蛋糕被扔進窗內，愛麗絲見機趕緊吞下一塊。跟她預測的一樣，她身體開始變小了。

等到她小到能通過門口，她就從房子溜了出去。

「我要把這些事情都記住。」愛麗絲跑著心中閃過這念頭。

「等到我回去學校，我要寫一篇長文，記敘這些怪事，還有身體偶爾……不對，是經常變大變小的狀況。」

「我還要寫說，變成九呎高的巨人，跟只有幾吋高的身高，會帶來的好處和壞處。不過，誰會相信我只需要吃吃這個，或喝喝那個，就可以自由變換自己的身高呢……？」

p. 52 就在此時，愛麗絲的面前出現了一隻巨大的小狗，身型比愛麗絲還龐大。大狗伸出了一隻腳掌，想要摸摸她。

情急之下，愛麗絲撿起旁邊的樹枝，卻發現它重得跟木頭一樣。愛麗絲用上渾身力氣，使勁把樹枝拋遠，想分散大狗的注意力。

大狗轉身躍向空中，高興地吠叫，追逐著掉落的樹枝。愛麗絲藉機逃跑。跑了好一段路後，她攤在小灌木叢旁緩口氣。

在確認自己安全後，她開始思量著：「我要長回正常的大小，我想去鐵門後的花園瞧一瞧。」她心意已決，四處尋找能放大身體的飲料瓶。

[第五章] 毛毛蟲的叮嚀

p. 54 愛麗絲走進了茂密的樹林，尋找能吃的食物。她發現了一朵蘑菇，就跟她的身高差不多大小。

她踮起腳尖，從菇傘邊緣偷偷望去，正好和在傘頂休息的毛毛蟲碰個正著。

「妳是誰？」毛毛蟲問。

「先生，我恐怕沒法回答這個問題，很抱歉。」愛麗絲說。

p. 56–57「妳為什麼不肯說？」毛毛蟲又問。

「因為我的身體變大變小的，今天一整天都這樣，我也搞不清楚自己是誰，好像怎麼說都不太對。」愛麗絲禮貌地解釋。

「那妳表演給我看。」毛毛蟲要求。

於是愛麗絲朗誦起一首舊詩作：

年長又行動緩慢的老師啊，但你的眼神炯炯有神。
我只需一眼，就能理解一篇長篇論文。
辯論使我們不再需要矯正鏡片，
因為它使我的視力不再腐壞。

年老又肥胖的上師啊，然你的四肢鬆散柔軟。
我的動作粗魯隨意。
瑜伽讓我心靈敏銳，身體靈巧，
雖然我吸引不了女人的目光。

年老又疲累的旅客啊，然你的心溫暖而開明。
我的馬車行經一路上的斷垣殘壁。
同理之心洗滌我的精神，救贖我的靈魂，
拯救人們的苦難。
我看著歷史的軌跡，我拭去絕望與黑暗，
我的心中滿懷喜樂，我的期盼如此安定。

p. 58–59 「妳的詩好像有點奇怪，有些字都改過了，是不是妳的腦袋一團亂？」毛毛蟲先生問。「再說妳到底是誰？」毛毛蟲又問了一遍。

「我之前以為我是愛麗絲，但我變大時，我又覺得自己像梅寶，結果我就不敢說自己是誰了，尤其我現在才這麼一丁點大。」愛麗絲努力向毛毛蟲解釋她目前的困境。

「所以妳從梅寶的身上看到了自己？」毛毛蟲問。

「不是，也不是這樣子。」愛麗絲自己也不大確定。

「所以，妳具有多重身分。」毛毛蟲先生以哲學家的口吻評論。

「妳感覺身體裡有另一個雙胞胎，這也不是件壞事，因為在妳短暫的生命中，無論遇到什麼事，都將有個同伴一直陪著妳。」

「梅寶！我的雙胞胎！還在我的身體裡！天啊！千萬不要！」愛麗絲驚恐地大叫。

「其實妳只是會變大又縮小而已，只要妳學會如何控制這力量，妳很快就會習慣的。」

「從這裡，這邊會讓妳變大，那邊則會讓妳變小。」毛毛蟲說。

「哪裡的這邊？哪裡的那邊？」愛麗絲問。

「蘑菇的兩邊。」只見毛毛蟲先生輕鬆地從蘑菇上彈下來，緩緩扭動著離開。

p. 60 和毛毛蟲分別後，愛麗絲從蘑菇兩邊各撕下一塊。她先嚐了其中一塊，想知道會發生什麼事。

愛麗絲的脖子開始伸長，越過了樹林，她甚至望見樹林的邊緣。「我的天啊！我的脖子跟蛇一樣長了！我看不到我自己的腳！也看不到我的手！」

「有條蛇想要偷走我的蛋，要謀殺我的寶寶！」鴿子媽媽大叫。「怎麼沒有頒布法令，禁止蛇不准越過樹頂？」

「鴿子媽媽，我不是蛇，我根本不吃生雞蛋啊。」愛麗絲大聲回應她。

p. 62-63 「蛋就是蛋，哪還有分什麼生的或熟的。只要妳喜歡蛋，妳就是蛇。」鴿子媽媽生氣地說。

「進化這東西真討厭，為什麼我有翅膀，妳身上卻長鱗片？我在電話線杆上築巢，妳的同類來靠近；我在劇院的壁架築巢，妳的同類也來靠近。」

「大自然的創意卻危害到我的後代，真是太不公平了！應該要頒布法令，讓你們這些蛇類不准靠近才對。」

氣憤難耐的鴿子媽媽想啄愛麗絲的眼睛，但她的動作太慢了，愛麗絲已經趁機吃下另一塊蘑菇，轉眼就縮回到了樹林中。

「我可以任意改變大小了。現在我只需要找到回美麗花園的路。」愛麗絲心想。

愛麗絲的五臟六腑又伸又縮地變形，全都攪在一起，不過能變回正常的大小讓她很高興。

「我可以先睡一下，反正我不趕時間。我需要休息一下，再想辦法去找那座美麗的花園。」

163

[第六章] 公爵夫人和笑臉貓

`p. 64` 愛麗絲沒找到花園，反而來到了一棟大房子前。她還在思考下一步時，就看到一名使者從樹林中跑出來，上前敲門。

愛麗絲感到很好奇，悄悄躲到樹叢後偷聽。

「皇后有令，請公爵夫人參加槌球比賽。」

一名男管家從屋裡出來，向使者說：「請出示你的身分！」

`p. 66–67` 使者露出自己的徽章，並回答：「我是紅心皇后派來的使者，我希望你能確實替我傳達訊息。」

男管家拉長了臉說：「你說什麼？你真傲慢無理，要知道，我的階級比你更高。」

「但我可是替皇后工作的，你跟我根本沒辦法比。我現在就要知道公爵夫人是否要參賽。」使者嚴肅地說。

「希望公爵夫人可以慎重考慮參賽一事，這樣才不會違背皇后的意旨。」

「那你就慢慢等吧。」男管家回答。

使者和管家身為皇家僕人，在表現勢利態度和矯作言語的比賽上，兩人互不相讓。因為彼此都互相瞧不起，把對方當作隱形人，站在原地動也不動。

突然，男管家低頭閃躲。原來從房裡射出了一只平底鍋，差點就擊中使者。使者害怕地跑開，尖聲大叫：「你想殺了我嗎？」

「你猜對了。」管家開始對使者窮追猛打。

「我再也不會到這鬼地方來。」

「我也不想再看到你。」

直到遠處，愛麗絲都還聽見兩人的爭執聲。

p. 68–69 愛麗絲小心翼翼地靠近門，打開門走進去。門通往一間寬敞的廚房，裡面有位廚師正在煮湯。她正翻箱倒櫃，忙著把各種調味料加進鍋爐裡。

公爵夫人膝蓋上有個嬰兒坐在旁邊，嬰兒一下發出嗚咽的哭聲，一下哇哇大叫。整間廚房充滿了胡椒的香氣。

愛麗絲開始打噴嚏，公爵夫人也是，就連哇哇叫的小嬰兒也不時打起噴嚏。

「你是誰？」公爵夫人問，然後又兇巴巴地説：「別吵了，你這隻豬！」

公爵夫人説到最後一個字時，音量忽然變很大，嚇得愛麗絲差點跳了起來。不過她隨即就明白那是對小嬰兒説的，不是在罵她。

「妳不要再亂加一堆胡椒了，巫婆，我和寶寶就不能好好休息嗎？」公爵夫人氣急敗壞地對女廚説。

「我辛辛苦苦只為了餵飽你們，妳現在竟然叫我巫婆，還真是感恩啊！」

p. 70 女廚開始朝公爵夫人和小嬰兒丟擲餐具，小嬰兒因為這樣哭鬧得更大聲了。一只平底鍋擦過小嬰兒的鼻子，差點把他打下來。

「妳在做什麼？」愛麗絲大喊。「哦！那是他寶貝的鼻子！」

好幾個盤子摔碎在愛麗絲的腳邊，她害怕地跳來跳去閃躲。

「這一定是要謀殺我的陰謀，因為這個巫婆，我的死期就快到了。妳抱著寶寶，起碼妳還關心他。我要趕快準備參加皇后的槌球比賽了。」

p. 72 公爵夫人说著，就回頭把小嬰兒丟進愛麗絲的懷中。她頭也不回地衝向門口，愛麗絲抱著小嬰兒在後面緊追著她。

「我不能把寶寶丟在那邊，她們沒多久就會把他殺掉的。」愛麗絲說。她懷中的嬰兒發出「咕嚕咕嚕」的聲音表示贊同。「別吵！」愛麗絲警告他。

小嬰兒又「咕嚕咕嚕」地叫了起來，愛麗絲低頭看著他的臉。讓她大吃一驚的是，嬰兒竟然變成了一頭豬！愛麗絲馬上把「他」放下，只見小豬快步跑進樹林中。

p. 74-75 愛麗絲走進森林，不久碰到一隻對著愛麗絲咧嘴而笑的柴郡貓，他正在樹幹上休息。

愛麗絲滿心狐疑地靠近他。「貓怎麼會笑呢？」她嘀咕著，不過他聽到了她的疑問，說：

「看來妳對貓不夠了解。我們都會笑，造物主賦予我們這種能力。當我們有感而發時，就會咧嘴微笑，就像在葬禮上時。」

「在葬禮上笑很不恰當，也沒禮貌。」愛麗絲說。

「胡說！」笑臉貓斷然回應。「是誰規定葬禮一定要合宜合禮的？」

「那現在有什麼讓你感觸良多的事嗎？」愛麗絲問。

「有啊，我深深感覺到了。因為不論接下來妳選擇哪條路，妳都會碰到瘋子。」笑臉貓做出了預言。

「是嗎？前方有『讓人發瘋』的病毒在傳染嗎？」她詢問。

愛麗絲想起剛才的胡椒、小豬，還有在公爵夫人廚房遇到的混亂情形。「你是說，你也是瘋子嗎？」

「是啊，我們都瘋了。既然妳現在在這裡，那妳也是瘋子，而且一定會發瘋。最終我們都將走上瘋狂一途。」笑臉貓面帶微笑解釋著。

　　「不對，我不同意！我又沒瘋，我也不想成為瘋子！」愛麗絲大喊。接著她露出了可愛笑容，問：「不管如何，請告訴我要走哪邊好嗎？」

　　「嗯，讓我說一張圖畫給妳看，包括每個方向妳會遇到什麼景物。」他回應。

　　「你說的話毫無邏輯可言。圖畫是用筆刷和五彩顏料創作出來的，才不是用抽象的文字。」愛麗絲批評。

　　 p. 76 　笑臉貓不理會愛麗絲的評論，他接著說：「往東邊走，妳會碰到三月兔；往西邊去，妳會找到帽商先生。他們兩個人有很嚴重的憂鬱症，都該去看看精神科。」

　　「三月兔的腦袋裝了很多天馬行空的點子，所以老是不自覺地說著愚蠢的話。」

　　愛麗絲感到好奇，她問：「什麼樣的點子啊？」

　　「很聰明的點子，像編織宇宙的布料、裁縫空間與時間的方式。三月兔想成為一位玄學家。不過呢，三月兔的瘋狂都是帽商先生造成的，因為他總想搞懂帽商先生的想法。」笑臉貓詳細解釋。

　　 p. 78 　「他老是在想事情？三月兔好像會計喔。」愛麗絲忍不住大笑。

　　「妳竟然嘲笑這麼悲傷的事情，目前還沒有方法醫治他們的病。我看除非精神病治療有重大突破，不然沒人可以消除他們的症狀。所以，妳可要仔細考量，慎重選出下條路。」笑臉貓嘴笑得更開了。

「嗯，現在是歡樂的五月，說不定三月兔在五月的春天不會那麼瘋狂，那我往東邊走。」愛麗絲做出了決定。

「那到時候見了。」笑臉貓說完便慢慢消失，從身體到頭，最後不見的是他的笑容。

[第七章] 瘋狂茶會

p. 80　愛麗絲在路上看到一座蘋果樹園。帽商、三月兔和一隻睡鼠坐在一棵大樹蔭下，三人圍著大桌子喝著茶。

「夥伴，親愛的朋友，過來跟我們多喝一點茶吧！這茶葉是有機的，味道真棒！」帽商邀請愛麗絲。

「我根本還沒喝，又怎麼能多喝一點？」愛麗絲就坐時回應他。

p. 82　「我向妳保證，妳一定會想多喝一點，不會想少喝一點。」帽商說，他順手將一堆茶杯上的茶壺放好。

愛麗絲有點猶豫。桌上的布巾沾到了醬漬，糖罐和果醬瓶看得到螞蟻爬進爬出。她覺得螞蟻窩一定藏在哪個餐具裡面。

此外，愛麗絲也不想移動茶壺，她怕底下堆好的茶杯會倒塌。

p. 84–85　「妳又沒什麼急事，好好休息一下，趕快幫自己倒點茶。」睡鼠催促著。

「我一點也不渴。」愛麗絲說。三人不滿意愛麗絲的答覆，全部盯著她瞧。他們的目光逼得愛麗絲趕快重申：「我不渴，真的！」

「妳該説出妳的心聲。」睡鼠堅定地勸説。

「我有，我想什麼就説什麼，我想的就是我説的。」愛麗絲用天真無邪的笑容回應，以掩飾自己的真心。

「是嗎？」睡鼠冷嘲熱諷地怪叫。「妳真的認為『我得到我喜歡的東西』跟『我喜歡我得到的東西』意思一樣嗎？

「妳也認為『我看到我吃的東西』跟『我吃我看到的東西』是相同的嗎？」帽商先生説。

「還是妳覺得『我睡覺時在呼吸』等於『我呼吸時在睡覺』呢？」三月兔又問。

三人十分享受炫耀自己的優越感，他們把愛麗絲當作消遣的娛樂。

愛麗絲不知該怎麼反駁他們。他們的桌子一團亂，他們的邏輯很充分，不過禮儀卻糟透了。

「這個果園很漂亮。」愛麗絲説，想換個話題。

「這塊地很棒，我張貼『出租糖蜜井』的廣告，一下子就被租走了。」帽商先生説。

p. 86 「糖蜜井在哪裡？」愛麗絲問。

「就在附近，沿著這條石子路走過去就會看到。」三月兔回答。

「也許有人會沉到這個井裡。」愛麗絲説。

「不會，大家都可以浮在上面。孕婦會像船一樣漂起來，像艾絲、緹莉和蕾西她們懷孕時，都是光著身子跳進井裡面。當然，她們還咯咯地笑。」帽商先生向愛麗絲解釋。

睡鼠還提到：「艾絲、緹莉和蕾西是藝術家，三人都偏好畫英文『M』開頭的事物，像是記憶（memory）、少數的（minor）、月光（moonlight）、貸款（mortgage）、母親（mother）和『很多』（muchness）等等。」

「『記憶』和『很多』沒辦法被畫出來。」愛麗絲打斷睡鼠的話。

「妳有和『記憶』或『很多』說過話嗎？」睡鼠質問她。

「當然沒有。」愛麗絲回答。

「所以妳不該多嘴！」睡鼠大罵。

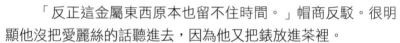

p. 88-89 愛麗絲不喜歡睡鼠的惡劣態度。顯然，這三個人都不適合再有進一步的對話。

愛麗絲想盡早離開他們越好，但此時她看見帽商先生吃著酸橙，將自己的錶放進茶裡。

「別這樣，很快你的錶就沒辦法看時間了！」」愛麗絲警告他。

「反正這金屬東西原本也留不住時間。」帽商反駁。很明顯他沒把愛麗絲的話聽進去，因為他又把錶放進茶裡。

「我說她在撒謊。一看就知道啦，一只不出聲喝茶的錶，或是任何自然現象像是漲漲退退的潮水，都沒法將時間留在岸邊。」三月兔自信滿滿地說。

帽商先生打了個大嗝，嘆了口氣說：「去年皇宮任命我替一件歷史事件譜曲，曲名就叫做《皇家婚禮 25 週年慶》。我在慶典上擔任主唱，可是皇后卻認為我在謀殺時間。」

「所以，我和『時間』的交情也終止了。『他』拋棄了我，躲到酸橙樹上睡覺去了。從此以後，時間就不理會我的要求了！所謂的時間，只有『酸橙時間』和『喝茶時間』。」

「你說『他』？他是誰？」愛麗絲問。

「時間。」帽商回答。「所以我們沒有時間洗茶具，還必須一下午待在戶外曬太陽。」

「所以，這個茶會永遠不會結束吧？」愛麗絲詢問。

p. 90–91 「是的，雖然可能沒什麼用，不過我建議：『永遠不要浪費時間。』」帽商先生若有所思地説。

「沒錯，事情確實沒什麼改變，我早該知道在皇后吃酸橙時高歌歡唱，會讓自己變成罪人。」

才説完，帽商先生、三月兔和睡鼠頭點上自己的茶杯睡著了。愛麗絲趁機從這場瘋狂茶會溜了出來。

[第八章] 皇后的槌球比賽

p. 92 終於，愛麗絲找到了一間有小鐵門的房間。她想用鑰匙開門，她先咬下一口蘑菇，讓自己縮小到適當的大小。

接著她把門打開，走進了美麗花園，置身於花團錦簇的花朵與清涼噴泉中。

「這裡真是太美了！」愛麗絲高興地呼吸著芬芳的空氣。有兩個貌似撲克牌的人正用油漆專心地彩繪玫瑰。

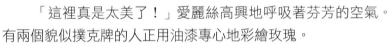

p. 94–95 「這邊到左半部的玫瑰你負責。」梅花五怪腔怪調地命令梅花三工作，「如果日落時分你還沒把玫瑰漆成紅色，我就把你砍頭。」

「不要模仿皇后的口音！你的頭還能留著，你就要偷笑了。」梅花三説。

一朵接著一朵，白色玫瑰在兩個撲克牌人優美靈巧的筆觸下，成了鮮紅的花朵。

「這個差事既無趣又丟臉。我可是個學者呢，從國王學院畢業的生物系學生，竟然拿著油漆刷，真是太可笑了！」梅花三説，「失去空氣，這些玫瑰不知道還能活多久？」

「我是物理學家，不清楚化學的光合作用，你才是這裡的生物學家。」梅花五回應。

「但是我是動物學家，不是植物學家呢。總之，我覺得要製造葉綠素不需要氧氣。」梅花三表示。

忽然，兩人神色慌張，停止了方才的對話。他們趴下來，將身體平貼在潮濕的土上，大喊：「恭迎皇后陛下！」

p. 96 皇家的紅心侍臣走在前頭，而盛大隊伍的最後則是國王和紅心皇后。

「妳是誰？」皇后詢問愛麗絲。

「我叫愛麗絲，陛下。」愛麗絲向皇后行禮自我介紹，皇后顯得相當滿意。

「愛麗絲，這位是紅心侍臣的核心外交使者，打聲招呼。」皇后命令。紅心傑克向愛麗絲點了點頭。

「過來加入我們的槌球比賽。」皇后命令愛麗絲，於是愛麗絲便跟著隊伍一起走。

皇家隊伍轉向走向運河旁的廣場。侍從遞給愛麗絲一隻紅鶴，當作比賽的球槌。

這隻紅鶴對愛麗絲來說有點太重了。所有的撲克牌人彎下身子，把自己當作球門，球則是用活生生的刺蝟。

「我從來沒看過那麼奇怪的槌球比賽。」愛麗絲心想。

p. 98 刺蝟不斷竄逃，不然就是被擊中馬上昏倒。

愛麗絲覺得用一隻活生生的動物，去攻擊另一隻動物很罪惡，她就是沒辦法拉長紅鶴的脖子當球槌打球。

皇后看到搞不定動物的選手，開始破口大罵。

一個幻影出現在半空中，發射出彩色的光芒。

那團光越來越大，愛麗絲皺起眉頭，直覺告訴她，自己就快要認出那飄動的彩色光球了。

p. 100-101 場上球員都聚集在漂浮的球體下方。它的光芒變得更刺眼，靜止在半空中，好像打算一直停在那裡。

光球變成了一顆毛球，原來是笑臉貓現出了部分身形，因為只看得見他的頭。

「砍了他的頭！」皇后大叫。「干擾比賽的人就要被砍頭。」

「但是這顆頭沒有連著身體，在這種不利的情況下，您沒辦法砍掉他的頭。」紅心傑克使者反駁皇后。

「你總是可以將不利的情況變得更不利。只要這個人有頭，就有辦法砍掉他的頭。」國王做出解釋，不理會紅心傑克的意見。

「這隻貓是公爵夫人的，也許你們該先和她談談。」愛麗絲想轉移大家的注意力，幫助笑臉貓脫困。

「不過公爵夫人現在在牢裡。」國王回應。

「沒關係，把她帶來！」皇后下令。愛麗絲接受了皇后的命令，在等待可以逃跑的時機。

p. 102 「我可憐的主人啊，被關進監獄了。」笑臉貓大聲咆哮，只聽見四下突然傳來旁觀者的驚訝聲。

「我的頭可安穩的呢！」笑臉貓說，雙眼像水晶球般炯炯有神。

「沒人殺得了我，除非我自己想死，當然了，希望我永遠不會，我可不像你們那麼瘋狂。」笑臉貓咧嘴大笑，便消失了。

［第九章］假海龜的故事

p. 104 從瘋狂的槌球賽逃走後，愛麗絲在路上碰到了公爵夫人。「我以為妳被關起來了！」愛麗絲驚呼。

公爵夫人回答：「我又沒犯什麼大罪。有時國王會仁慈地赦免要被砍頭的民眾，之後妳就會知道了。」

然後公爵夫人看到愛麗絲身上的紅鶴：「希望這鶴吃起來不像芥末。我重新訂了廚房規約：不准使用胡椒！當然，芥末也不行。」

p. 107 愛麗絲忍不住懷疑，公爵夫人也許能分辨胡椒和芥末，但她真能搞清楚植物和鳥類的差別嗎？

公爵夫人滔滔不絕地說著：「就像憲法一樣，我會在廚房嚴格執行這項規定。創造一個有條不紊的廚房，是我的新理想。我也不需要請員工了，因為以新規定來管理廚房，非常有效率。我會辭去廚子，畢竟她年紀大了，也該退休了。」

大部分的時間都是公爵夫人在說話，甚至對自己的理念長篇大論。

不過公爵夫人的談話對愛麗絲而言，只是一堆無意義的文字組合而已。「或許公爵夫人可以試著把話都寫下來，這樣她的聽眾會更了解她的意思。如果她有東西可以讓我讀，我也能了解她在說什麼。」愛麗絲心想。

p. 108 突然之間，皇后不知從何處出現了！她雙手環抱胸前，對公爵夫人發出警告：「快滾，不然我就砍了妳的頭！」

公爵夫人飛也似地逃離現場。接著皇后轉向愛麗絲，也對她做出了警告。

「回來繼續打槌球，不然妳也要掉腦袋！」愛麗絲只好跟著皇后回到比賽場上。

場上的選手看到皇后陛下到來都十分慌張。沒過多久，除了愛麗絲、國王和紅心使節之外，所有人都被皇后囚禁起來。顯然，皇后非常渴望拿到槌球比賽冠軍。

許多可貴的生命正因皇后的野心而遭險，眾囚犯紛紛求饒。

所幸，這個危急的情況為時不久，很快就解決了。國王有時會生起崇高的道德感，便熱衷於釋放囚犯。就在皇后離開後，他馬上就赦免了所有人。

p. 110-111 不知為何，皇后帶愛麗絲來到一頭半獅半鷲的怪獸旁。獅鷲獸是奇怪的生物，因為牠的頭是老鷹，身體卻是獅子。

獅鷲獸倏地張開了雙眼，盯著愛麗絲看。皇后命令怪獸帶愛麗絲到宮外的一處隔絕之所，去見假海龜先生。

愛麗絲丟下紅鶴，因為牠很重不好攜帶。愛麗絲跟著怪獸通過兩顆大石中的夾縫，在懸崖邊找到了海龜先生。

假海龜先生是個說故事高手。外面流傳著他是世上最傷心的人。

「我難過，是因為我想回家，但是為何你看來如此悲傷呢？」愛麗絲問。

「親愛的，」假海龜先生開始述說自己的故事。「從前從前，我是隻真海龜，我和同學在海中學校上課。一些優秀老師教了我們很多事，我的啟蒙老師是隻老烏龜，我們都叫他『陸龜先生』。」

「如果他是隻真海龜，你們為什麼還稱他叫陸龜（Tortoise）？」愛麗絲問。

「我們這樣叫他，是因為老師慢慢地教我們（taught us）。緩慢教學是他的專業。」傷心的海龜說。

p. 112–113 怪獸發出一個怪聲，彷彿在抗議愛麗絲的提問。

　　「安靜點，怪獸先生！」假海龜厲聲斥責他。他繼續說著故事：「在以前，傳統學校重視的是音樂和法語，不過只有我們學校比較特別，我們學的是洗東西。」

　　「但是假海龜先生，你就住在海裡，你根本不需要洗東西啊。」愛麗絲提出質問。「更何況，你也不用穿衣服，你身上已經有殼了，你需要洗什麼東西嗎？」

　　「殼就是我們的衣服啊。我有可更換的殼，還有要洗的髒殼，就跟你平常換洗髒衣服一樣。」假海龜先生替自己辯解。

　　「我們受的是最好的教育，學的是不同流派的算術。你知道，像是『野心』、『分心』、『醜陋』和『嘲弄』。」怪獸說，他急著想炫耀自己同時學習這麼多困難的科目以博得尊敬。

　　「『醜陋』要怎麼計算？你是要說『乘法』嗎？」愛麗絲努力想理解。

　　「妳還真死腦筋。醜陋就是美麗的反面啊。」怪獸不耐煩地解釋。

p. 114–115 「那你要怎麼計算美麗？」愛麗絲又問。

　　「真是丟臉！妳不要再干擾我了！不准再問一些無禮又無聊的問題！」怪獸大聲說著，責備愛麗絲不該隨便找麻煩，臉上表情很猙獰。

　　假海龜先生繼續說他的故事。「教戲劇的螃蟹教我們古典學裡『笑（laughing）和悲傷（grieving）』的課程。螃蟹老師特別擅長『剛強』和『暴躁』的部分，他的帶課方式也很嚴格。」

　　「那螃蟹是現代文學的嚴厲評論家，尤其是針對浪漫主義小說的分析。」怪獸補充。

假海龜先生以悲傷的聲調繼續講故事。「第一天去學校，我們上了十個鐘頭的課，第二天只有九個鐘頭，第三天剩下八個鐘頭……。」

「為什麼你們每過一天，就少上一個鐘頭的課啊？」愛麗絲打斷。

「上課（lesson）之所以叫上課，就是因為課會越上越少（lessen）。」怪獸瞪著愛麗絲，不耐煩地解釋。（註：lesson 和 lessen 讀音相同，但字義分別是「課程」及「減少」。）

愛麗絲心想，如果以這種速度減少課程的話，那到了第十一天，就會沒課可上了。她小聲地表示，第十一天應該是假日。

［第十章］龍蝦的方塊舞

p. 116 「我們來教她跳舞吧。」怪獸先生提議。

「天啊！我一直盼望著有天我們可以再跳一次超棒的龍蝦方塊舞。」難過的假海龜哽咽著說。

「我知道小步舞曲怎麼跳。」愛麗絲興奮的說。

「這兩種舞步有著細微的不同。」假海龜解釋。「我甚至替龍蝦們做好了一首返家之詩。」

「但龍蝦被視為放逐者，所以沒有出版社回應我討論出版的事，禁令指出不得和遷徙中的龍蝦有任何交談。」

p. 118–119 「這裡的龍蝦人數是不是很少？」愛麗絲問。

「他們全走光了，沒有龍蝦留在這裡。」假海龜先生快哭了。

「這裡是他們的原生地，但是他們還是走了。」怪獸先生也很感傷，「皇后是一位激進的改革資本家，她上任後頒布了新的經濟政策，嚴格強迫人民遵守。」

　　「皇后很快就籌措到許多資金。凡是沒有遵從她指令的龍蝦，她都處以死刑。新政中的一項首要策略，就是她將逮捕到的龍蝦作成機械玩具。」

　　許多龍蝦都感受到自己的危險處境，為了躲避皇后的瘋狂新政，也想住保項上人頭，所以便索性離開了。

　　皇后一心想推行經濟政策來獲利，也成了她主要的心結。

p. 120-121 假海龜開始朗誦自己的詩作：

> 皇家的法令，
> 至高無上皇后的資本主義，
> 全新的奇怪經濟，
> 消滅了她的仇敵。
>
> 龍蝦反抗者誕生，
> 喔！他毫不畏懼，
> 人們稱他反叛英雄提頓
>
> 龍蝦子民向偉大的革命者提頓
> 宣示他們的忠心。
> 龍蝦們出海去，
> 誓言「找到回家的路！」
>
> 皇后的經濟政策快速崩塌，
> 一切早被勝利的反叛英雄提頓猜透，
> 他說「好人才有好報」。

難過的假海龜長嘆一口氣，接著說：「大批的龍蝦離去帶來了絕大的災難。我想在我有生之年，都沒法再跳一次龍蝦方塊舞了。」

　　怪獸先生試著正向思考，他便說：「有傳言說，有新的方塊舞在其他島上流行，而且各地都可以看到龍蝦身影。」

　　愛麗絲正好也聽膩了龍蝦的悲慘故事，她開心地提議：「我們來跳舞吧！」

　　「是啊，我們來跳舞！海龜來做我們的指揮官。」怪獸先生說。

p. 122–123 海龜先生卻拒絕：「可是沒有海豚（porpoise）陪我。我需要一隻『海豚』來幫我發號施令。」
「你是要說『目標』（purpose）嗎？」愛麗絲問。（註：porpoise 和 purpose 兩字的讀音相似。）

　　「我的意思是，一個沒有海豚幫忙的指揮官，只會讓舞步變得很混亂，因為沒有人聽得懂指揮官的指令。」難過的海龜解釋。

　　「我可以幫你，來吧。」怪獸先生請求道。

　　假海龜先生轉身告訴愛麗絲：「我們只能大概教妳一下這神奇舞蹈的感覺。」

　　「首先，除了自貝殼進化的物種外，所有的生物都在海岸邊排排站。」海龜先生讓愛麗絲和怪獸先生和他站在同一直線上。

　　怪獸先生解釋說：「接著，指揮官就會大喊：『嘻哈』，然後那一排的人就要回應他的口號。」

　　「嘻哈！」假海龜大喊。

　　「嘻哈！」愛麗絲和怪獸一起回應。

「然後抓著一隻龍蝦，擠壓他的身體，扭轉他的尾巴。再往前行進兩步。」假海龜發號司令。

愛麗絲和怪獸聽令動作。

p. 124-125 「接著，把龍蝦丟進海裡，等著他像飛彈一樣『咻』地衝出海面。接著游到那隻龍蝦身邊，抓住他，重複做一遍剛才的動作，然後翻身返回岸邊。」假海龜命令。

愛麗絲和怪獸照著海龜的話行動。

假海龜接著又說：「聽到指揮官喊出『邪惡的鉗子』時，互相交換龍蝦。現在準備好了嗎？『邪惡的鉗子！』」

假海龜一聲令下，愛麗絲和怪獸優雅輕鬆地把手上的隱形甲殼動物交給對方。

「現在用妳交換來的這隻龍蝦來配合。」海龜先生深吸一口氣，有點上氣不接下氣。

「這支舞學起來還真累人。」愛麗絲說。她也喘個不停。

「這支舞的目的就在於運動到妳的全身肌肉。」假海龜解釋，「等到舞跳完，妳就好像玩了一場槌球比賽。」

「紅心傑克的審判要開始了。」有人在遙遠的那頭喊著。

「我們去看看！」怪獸先生喊道，愛麗匆忙緊跟在後面，隨著他前往皇家法庭。

[第十一章] 誰偷走了餡餅

p. 126 審判在皇宮內舉行。皇后神情彆扭，坐在王位上，後方擺著正義女神雕像。

一盤餡餅放在正中央的桌上。這個神奇國度的所有人潮，全聚集在皇宮附近。比爾蜥蜴和會議式賽跑的成員是這次審理的陪審團。

愛麗絲沒辦法靠近那看起來很可口的餡餅，因為中間隔著陪審員席。他們就像是一堵牆，擋住了她和餡餅。

p. 128-129 國王進入會場，四下響起一片掌聲。白兔先生是法庭的傳令官，他大聲宣布：「法庭內請安靜！」隨後他拿起一張紙宣讀：「紅心傑克偷走了皇后的餡餅。」

　　「你們的裁定是？」國王詢問陪審團。

　　「不，不，不，國王陛下！別急著做裁定！應該先對證人進行口頭交叉審問，不然外面對我們宮廷的風評會很差，我們要維持形象才行，有很多報社的記者也到場了呢。」白兔先生說。「傳公爵夫人的廚子。」

　　「我已經向公爵夫人請辭了。」老廚子走進來時說。在場的人都打起噴嚏，因為她身上有胡椒味。

　　國王打了幾個好大的噴嚏，最後終於提出詢問：「妳知道被偷走的餡餅嗎？」

　　愛麗絲疑惑地看著桌上的餡餅，「但是餡餅就在這裡啊？」她大喊。

　　「我不是在問妳，小女孩！廚子，馬上回答我。」國王下令。

p. 130-131 「我什麼都不知道。我根本沒注意到餡餅。我是負責煮湯的，不是做餡餅的。」女廚回答。

　　「餡餅被偷的時候妳人在哪裡？」國王又問。

　　「我正在買東西。我看到藥草的春季目錄出來了，所以很興奮。我現在要自己開店，可以幫蜥蜴動手術，另外我還經營大黃的苗圃。」比爾蜥蜴聽聞公爵夫人前女廚的計畫後顫抖不已。

　　「好，妳可以走了。」國王讓前廚師離開後，發出命令：「傳下一位證人！」

「傳帽商！」白兔先生大喊。

「為什麼那個謀殺時間的傢伙還活著？」皇后生氣地咆哮。

「一宗罪歸一宗罪，好嗎？」國王打斷她。

「我……我只是個……可……可憐的老百姓，我……我……學得很少……根本不知道什麼……什麼……餡……餡餅。」帽商結結巴巴地說著，想方設法惹惱皇后。

「你不太會說話，需要好好矯正，你都結巴了。好了，你走吧。」國王讓帽商離開。

帽商先生離開的時候，偷偷抓了三塊餡餅。他小聲跟愛麗絲說：「我有三塊餡餅可以配茶，可是妳卻什麼都沒有。」

「我獲准去搜尋紅心傑克的私人物品，在廁所的工具箱找到了這張白紙。」白兔先生表示。他看起來像是個偵探、警官、律師，同時還是法庭傳令官。

p. 132-133 「白紙可以用來記錄或寫信。肅靜！讓我好好思考一下這項新證據。」國王沉默下來，現場的氣氛變得令人激動。

「哈哈！這張紙正好成為我處死餡餅小偷的最好利證。」皇后激動地說。「你沒有在上面簽名，代表你想隱藏自己是罪人，找不到你的字跡剛好吻合這項說法。」

「但是這本來就是一張白紙啊。」紅心傑克大喊。

皇后不耐煩地尖聲大叫，「你這封信是要寄給誰的？誰在跟你通信？這場判決非同小可，為什麼有人沒經過我的同意，就可以自由進入王室的廚房？一定是陰謀，有邪惡的體制想摧毀我們國家的經濟。策劃這場可怕陰謀的間諜，想要偷走所有的甜點，徹底打擊國家預算不足的困境。」

可憐的紅心傑克想替自己辯解：「但是我不是……」

「你們策劃行動的總部在哪裡？」皇后十分生氣，只見她呼吸急促，胸口隨之來回上下起伏不定。「罪證確鑿，沒有同謀人，再狡辯也沒用了。」

「那就結案吧。」國王告訴陪審團。「在我宣布你們退席之前，請先將這個罪大惡極的人繩之以法吧。」

p. 134-135 「馬上將這個間諜判刑！」皇后大叫，「除了砍頭，其他的刑責完全不用考慮。」

「不行！怎麼可以還沒聽取陪審團判決結果，就把人定罪呢？」愛麗絲大喊。

「怎麼不行？我們身為民主的一員，除了政教分離之外，連罪行裁定和判刑都是分開的。這兩者不需同時存在，這才是真正的民主。」皇后像平常一樣，高傲地解釋。

「這樣的程序更有效率，因為必須要準確做出決定，沒辦法事後再進行商議。每件案子的判決都是依罪行的輕重而論，所以判決就是『如判決所指，有罪』，這是每個人都知道的。」

愛麗絲開始對這場奇怪的審判失去耐心，她轉頭向一旁的怪獸先生說：「他們根本沒有證明出什麼，既然沒有實證，就應該宣判無罪釋放啊。」

愛麗絲說話的同時，她的身體開始慢慢變大。「為什麼？我沒有吃蘑菇，也沒有喝下任何東西啊？」她心想。

[第十二章] 愛麗絲的證詞

p. 136 「還有一位證人，國王陛下。」白兔先生提醒國王，然後大喊：「傳愛麗絲。」

愛麗絲起身，撞倒了旁邊一群陪審員。

在場的人都嚇到了。「什麼讓那女孩變成巨人的？」皇后驚呼。

「法庭第 47 條守則，超過一哩高的人，不可出席做證人。這是最古老的條例。」國王説。

「如果這是最古老的條例，它也應該是第一條才對。」愛麗絲説。「再説，我才沒有一哩那麼高。」

「沒人有規定最古老的條例就該是第一條。我本身是律師，制定了司法系統，我很了解何謂最古老的條例。」國王回應。

p. 138 「那你就應該知道全世界的案件，都必須等陪審團判決出來後，才進行定罪。」愛麗絲反駁，她覺得有義務要澄清法庭的程序。

「藐視法庭！為了維持皇家紀律，馬上砍了這女怪物的頭。」皇后命令。

就在同時，愛麗絲已經變得比週遭所有人都高大了，於是她勇敢表示：「我才不怕你們呢，你們只不過是一堆紙牌罷了！」

此番話激怒了撲克牌士兵，他們準備要對愛麗絲展開攻擊。就在下個瞬間，現場開始了一陣混亂攻勢。

橘色和粉紅色的火焰不斷射出，所有的撲克牌擺出鋒利的紙牌邊緣，衝向愛麗絲……。

p. 140–141 愛麗絲睜開雙眼，在河岸邊的青草地上醒來。姊姊還在一旁讀著書。

「我剛剛夢到了一個奇妙的國度呢！」愛麗絲興奮地説。

「妳看太多電影了吧。」姊姊微笑著説。

「真是個不可思議的夢！」愛麗絲驚叫，「夢裡的時代和現在不同，但是卻又感覺很熟悉。我知道這是虛構的，不過卻非常真實，好刺激喔！」

愛麗絲拍拍裙子上的落葉，向姊姊娓娓道來夢境的細節。一旁的蜥蜴悠閒地享受夕陽的餘暉，夕陽掛在天上像極了發光的粉橘圓盤。

栩栩如生的夢境，讓愛麗絲花了一些時間才重新適應現實。傍晚時分，她跟著姊姊回家時，心中有了一個想法──她要把這次的奇遇寫成故事。

隔天星期六下午，愛麗絲和姊姊到了當地教堂。

貼在教堂門口公布欄的傳單，要徵召日間照護中心的義工。

愛麗絲的年紀太小，不符合申請的規定，因此無法登記為正式義工，不過教堂人員很歡迎她「非正式的幫忙」。

p. 142 兩個人笑容滿面地離開教堂。愛麗絲拿著非正式義工的申請收據，覺得她將迎接另一個全新的冒險。

她沿著人行道跳起舞來，所有路旁的聲音與顏色都瞬間融合為一體，隨著她搖晃擺動，就像展開了一場虛幻的演奏會。頭頂的電線傳送著訊號。

不知道它們是否也帶來了奇幻世界居民的最新消息？

愛麗絲的腦海中浮現一個個奇妙的景象與人物，相信過不了多久，她又會有新的神秘旅程故事可說了。

p. 144 姊姊看著愛麗絲跳舞，想到她提過的故事。她深信愛麗絲將來會成為一位偉大的作家──一位構思出動人故事的作者。

沒錯，愛麗絲會永遠是個聰明又可愛的小女孩，她筆下趣味盎然的故事，將激發全世界所有好奇讀者的想像力。

Answers

Chapter 1

P. 11   **1** T

        2 A

P. 14   **3** F It was too difficult for Alice to make a curtsy while falling.

P. 19   **4** F What was inside the bottle was not alcohol.

        5 She ate a small piece of cake.

Chapter 2

P. 20   **1** A large fan.

P. 23   **2** A

P. 25   **3** She used Mr. Rabbit's large fan to fan herself.

P. 27   **4** F Alice survived from drowning by clambering up on the back of a mouse.

P. 29   **5** Dinah was Alice's cat, and she kept rodents away from Alice.

P. 31   **6** T

Chapter 3

P. 35   **1** The first "dry" is the opposite of "wet," and the second one is the opposite of "interesting."

        2 They listened to the beginning of a dry story, and then Ms. Dodo suggested doing some sports.

P. 37   **3** F Ms. Dodo declared that they were all winners of the race.

P. 41   **4** B

P. 43   **5** Because they were all afraid of Dinah, Alice's cat.

Chapter 4

Chapter 5

Chapter 6

Chapter 10

Chapter 11

Chapter 12

愛麗絲夢遊仙境【二版】
Alice's Adventures in Wonderland

作者 _ Lewis Carroll
改寫 _ Norman Fung
審訂 _ Dennis Le Boeuf / Liming Jing
翻譯 _ 鄭家文
編輯 _ 鄭家文／黃朝萍
協力編輯 _ 洪巧玲
校對 _ 賴祖兒
封面設計 _ 林書玉
排版 _ 葳豐／林書玉
製程管理 _ 洪巧玲
發行人 _ 周均亮
出版者 _ 寂天文化事業股份有限公司
電話 _ +886-2-2365-9739
傳真 _ +886-2-2365-9835
網址 _ www.icosmos.com.tw
讀者服務 _ onlineservice@icosmos.com.tw
出版日期 _ 2020年5月 二版一刷（250201）
郵撥帳號 _ 1998620-0 寂天文化事業股份有限公司

國家圖書館出版品預行編目資料

愛麗絲夢遊仙境 / Lewis Carroll 原著；Norman
Fung 改寫 . -- 二版 . -- 臺北市：寂天文化, 2020.04
　　面；　公分 . -- (Grade 5 經典文學讀本)
譯自：Alice's adventures in wonderland
ISBN 978-986-318-908-4(25K 平裝附光碟片)

1. 英語　2. 讀本

805.18　　　　　　　　　　　　　109004150